Frenemies by Destiny

Who you love and who loves you back
determines so much in your life.

—Lang Laev

One pursues a synthesis based on a belief
that a conflict is the result
of an order that is as yet unknown.

—Matthew Frederick & Vikas Mehta

Frenemies by Destiny

stories by
Soramimi Hanarejima

First Montag Press E-Book and Paperback Original Edition November 2018

Copyright © 2018 by Soramimi Hanarejima

As the writer and creator of this story, Soramimi Hanarejima asserts the right to be identified as the author of this book.

Montag Press
ISBN: 978-1-940233-60-4
Cover art © 2018 Rose Wong
Design © 2018 Rick Febré

Montag Press Team:
Project Editor — Mara Korzen
Managing Director — Charlie Franco

A Montag Press Book
www.montagpress.com
Montag Press
1066 47th Ave. Unit #9
Oakland CA 94601 USA

Montag Press, the burning book with the hatchet cover, the skewed word mark and the portrayal of the long-suffering fireman mascot are trademarks of Montag Press.

Printed & Digitally Originated in the United States of America
10 9 8 7 6 5 4 3 2 1

This book is a work of fiction. Names, characters, places, and incidents are either products of the author's vivid and sometimes disturbing imagination or are used fictitiously without any regards with possible parallel realities. Any resemblance to actual persons, living or dead, events, or locales is entirely coincidental.

Table of Contents

Starting Point

Without warning, everyone who knows me starts addressing me with a new nickname— essentially my name minus the *t* in it. It happens first in the office, and I conclude that the team is just trying out a new diminutive for me, which isn't an uncommon practice. Last week, Ruloftiq became Ruloq, then R-Prime. He's a good sport about it and even seems to enjoy having an ever-shifting soubriquet.

But soon, I'm receiving personal emails written with my name sans *t*, from out-of-state friends who, as far as I'm aware, have no connection with anyone at work. And when I meet with friends after work for book club, they too address me the same way.

So I check my name, and sure enough, the *t* is missing. Then I know this could only be your doing. You've long thought my name sounds warmer this way.

"You removed the *t* from my name, didn't you?" I accuse during a break in cooking class the next day, while we're waiting for the banana cake to cool.

"Yes, but, *admit it.* There's a certain undeniable appeal to it," you retort, shaking a whipped-cream-smeared spatula at me.

Fortunately, none of the sweet, white fluff is flung upon my garments while I'm taking today's session apronless.

"Whether or not it's appealing, that's beside the point," I refocus the discussion. "You can't just change someone's name without asking."

"You're not just *someone.*"

That remark throws me, leaving me simply half-glowering,

half-gaping at you and the spatula angled in my direction.

"You keep putting off things that you really should try," you continue. "To the extent that you need someone to get you to do these things."

I'm tempted to deny this, but I know that doing so would be taking a treacherously tenuous position.

"Yeah, you're right," I relent, though it feels like I've mentally conceded to you decades ago.

"Give it a chance. Don't merely dismiss it as not being your name," you urge.

I nod.

"Names don't have to be just the way they are. They can be starting points, for interesting variations or what have you. Like recipes. You don't have to follow them exactly."

Suddenly and inexplicably, this prompts me to wrest the spatula from your hands and lick the whipped cream from it. I find this very satisfying as you recoil in surprise.

Who You Will Be Meets Who I Am

Downtown, amid the urban bustle of pedestrians briskly moving through the stinging winter cold like they each have somewhere they need to be, I catch a glimpse of someone who resembles you in appearance and demeanor but has an air of calm maturity. I step aside, leaving the oncoming stream of city folk I was just navigating. My gaze returns to this doppelgänger at the end of the block, looking around—*just* looking around. Eyes keenly observant, yet relaxed. A posture of quiet readiness. The similarity is uncanny. And I realize this must be your future self, from my temporal perspective.

Walking towards this further-developed you, I become more and more certain that it is you from some future date.

"What are you doing here? You're not supposed to be here—now," I whisper to who you will become. "Unless it's an *emergency*. Is it an emergency?" I ask, growing concerned.

"Relax," your future self says. "I was just feeling nostalgic."

"You're here because of *nostalgia*?" I blurt, taken aback by your temporal tourism, somehow managing to keep my voice down. "You're going to create a temporal branching because of your nostalgia? And now you're never going to get back to when you came from."

"Actually, we've... solved that problem. I can't tell you the details of the theory and implementation. And I'll have to disrupt your memory after this to minimize the effects of this visit."

I note that your future voice is much like your voice now but more worldly and deliberate. Intriguing as it is, this observation doesn't stop me from taking issue with what's been revealed to me thus far.

"So if you're going to prevent me from remembering this, why can't you just explain it to me?" I ask.

"Because telling you too much could still... have some... undesirable effects."

"Because the memory disruption isn't totally perfect?"

"I can't really talk about that."

"So what can you talk about?"

"Almost anything else not related to the future."

"Even though it might not be our—my future?"

"I can't get into that."

"Okay, well, how are you doing then?"

"Oh, pretty good," future you answers with chipper normalcy.

"I guess you can't really tell me what you're up to."

"In the future? Nope. Sorry."

"Well, what about here? What are you doing here?"

"Enjoying things as they used to be."

"So it won't be like this in the future?"

"No."

"Wait, how come you could answer that question?"

"Because that answer isn't so... revealing. I mean, you really don't think it's going to be like this." Your future self opens your future arms to the cityscape about us. "Forever, did you?"

"Well, no," I answer.

The future self's hands withdraw from the grand gesture back into the warmth of coat pockets.

"But I thought some things would endure," I add.

"Oh, well, definitely, some things will."

"So you just can't tell me which ones—like, no details?"

"Pretty much."

"Okay."

"Yeah."

"So what have you done here?"

"I went to the bookstores that I liked."

"There aren't bookstores in the future?"

"No, not like the ones in your now."

My brow furrows with confusion.

"Wait," I say, holding up a gloved hand. "How come you could answer that question too?"

"Oh come *on*, you already know print publishing has been facing significant challenges. The paradigm has been in question for a while. All signs of a… transition have been made apparent to you."

"Okay. Still, it's hard to imagine a world without these kinds of bookstores."

"Or stores, for that matter."

"Stores aren't like this in the future?" I ask, incredulous. Sure, the nature of commerce is changing, but such a radical transformation seems at least decades off.

"Not necessarily," your future self says with hints of carefulness. "I'm just saying: it's hard for you to imagine a world without your usual fixtures. But maybe you should."

I nod at this nugget of commentary and advice.

"Well, while we're here together, you want to go ice skating? I was planning to do that too."

"Okay."

"Because ice is *so last decade* in my now," your future self says, laughing.

I think it's supposed to be a joke, and though I am laughing too, I am slightly unnerved by those words.

"It's too bad I'm not going to remember any of this," I say as we glide and scuff around the little frozen pond in the park downtown.

"Well, when I meet your future self in my now, I'll tell her about this," the future self says.

"Cool. I guess that's the next best thing."

"Yeah. It'll be nice to talk about it."

Then we're quiet as we continue to sail upon the ice.

Then the future of you says, "Let's go to that community music studio after this."

"Sure, that'll be nice. There's nothing like music to really make you feel like you're back in the good old days," I reply with imaginary extrapolation.

"Exactly."

"Have you already seen who you used to be?" I have to ask.

"Yes, from a distance. Briefly."

"Was that weird?"

"A little. It was nice too. I like this former self of mine."

"Me too."

"You'll like me even more."

"So you just get better with time?"

"Mostly."

I hope I will too. And our relationship as well. I want to ask about those things too, but I don't feel confident enough to, afraid that maybe the answers will disappoint or even demoralize me. Your future self probably can't answer such questions anyways.

So enough about the future, I decide. I should just enjoy these moments we share. After all, soon, it'll be as if they never happened.

Unexpected Visitor

Your imaginary friend absconds to my mind.

Fortunately, she does this while I'm lounging in the solarium on my day off. I doubt I'd be as hospitable to a mental runaway if I were at the office.

"We all need a change of setting once in a while," she tells me.

The mental hologram she's created of herself then reclines upon the sofa opposite the one I'm in.

I always thought of your imagination as the epitome of a changing setting, a realm ever permuting into new dreamscapes. But maybe that's what she needs a respite from: the always dynamic world of your mind.

"Well, I was about to listen to some pink noise," I say, pointing at the compact lacquer box on the little table between us.

"*Oh*, I've never tried that before," she says with glee.

The late-morning sunlight from the wide window to her right seems to illuminate even her voice. And like her words, she casts no shadow on the hardwood floor. She has never liked shadows.

"This sound spectrum is wondrously relaxing, but will it adversely affect you?" I ask.

Your imaginary friend just says, "I'll probably be fine."

"Okay, well, if anything happens, we can stop. Just let me know," I tell her, just in case.

"Yup."

I lean forward and open the box of pink noise, and the

familiar, tranquilizing hiss fills the air. I recline fully upon the fine leather of the sofa and let my body go limp as my experience of the world begins to dissolve. The conceptual boundaries that divide sky, mountain and window frame, floor, furniture and walls, chair cushions, me and the air, all these cognitive edges blur.

She starts to disappear, imaginary body growing ever more transparent, but she doesn't seem to mind.

When she's little more than a pair of eyes, I have to ask, "Are you okay?"

"Yes," she assures me, blinking.

"Okay," I murmur.

As most of my thoughts vanish, I feel like the world around me simply is. Like my mind has relinquished all but its most rudimentary interpretation of what I perceive, forming the most minimal comprehension of reality. This soon expands to my experience of self, until I feel that I barely yet quintessentially am.

This mode of being continues on until the contents of the box has been exhausted. The lulling sound thins as the last of it drifts out the windows I've left open for ventilation, and slowly, the world takes on familiar form. Like comprehensible reality is crystallizing out of sheer everythingness.

When I can see the sofa in front of me as a sofa again, I look for her eyes. But as much as I scrutinize the sofa, I see nothing remotely resembling eyes there.

Panic jerks me into an upright position. My breath quickens.

Have I dissolved away your imaginary friend into the aether of forgotten thoughts?

Looking and listening intently, I comb sight and sound for some vestige of her: an eyelash, a sigh, a glimmer of iris—anything I can lock my attention on to anchor her reimagining.

Then come the words, "That was fun," from a soft, wavering voice.

"*Oh man,*" I shout. "Are you okay? I was so worried."

"Yes, your fear really gave me a jolt. I'm touched that you care so much. Or would the guilt of banishing me to oblivion just be too much for your conscience to bear?"

"Please, no discussion about the relative proportions of selfish and selfless concern right now," I answer hurriedly, heart still racing. "I'm just glad you're fine."

Then I see her eyes looking in my direction, dreamily defocused. Relieved, I slump forward, elbows pressing into my knees, hands holding up my head. I watch as she starts to fuzzily and translucently regain form on the sofa.

"What else were you planning to do today?" she asks.

"I don't know," I answer slowly. "I need to recollect my thoughts after that mind-numbing episode."

"Yes, I feel your consciousness still sorting itself out."

I nod.

"Maybe I can check out your daydreams later," she suggests.

"Yeah, sure. There's no shortage of those."

"So I've heard. Maybe we should have lunch first. You're hungry, like a bear after hibernation."

Turning my attention to my physiological sensations, I find that indeed, my stomach is declaring its emptiness. I wonder what else she can tell me about myself. Perhaps the secrets my unconscious withholds from me?

Then I see that she's smiling at me, knowingly.

The Intimacy of Anonymity

This morning, I see you in the distance, walking down the boardwalk that crosses our neighborhood marsh.

Great, I think. *Now I can tell you about that amazing hologram in the Orthereal Woods.*

But when I cup my hands around my mouth to call out your name, I find it's just not there in my mind. And this isn't one of those tip-of-the-tongue moments. Not at all. Instead, your name seems far away, remote to the point of being absent. Like it's been ferried off to some nook in the landscape by amnesia's less aggressive but more infuriating little sibling.

Flabbergasted, I let my hands fall to my sides, and I simply watch you walk down those wooden planks until the reeds hide you from view.

Later in the day, you tell me about upcoming travel plans while we sit at a corner table in the yogurt bar, and even face to face with you, your name still feels out of reach, beyond my apprehension. Yet everything else about my comprehension of you seems normal. Your appearance and voice are as familiar as ever, and my other memories of you seem intact. It's just your name that eludes me. So I assume whatever's going on is only temporary.

But the inability to recall your name persists through the day and into the next, during which it disquiets my hours in the office. The absence of your name in my mind unnerves me, sporadically prompting everything from rational speculation to amorphous dread.

Unsettled that I seem to have no knowledge of your name,

I worry that something serious has happened or is happening to me. Am I in the early stages of a condition that will one day make it impossible for me to put names to things?

I attend my afternoon meetings in a state of thorough preoccupation, vacillating between the resolve and reluctance to see my metaphysiologist, interrogated at length by my concerns and curiosities. Would an appointment to discuss this matter be worth the copay? Might such an appointment be premature or an overreaction? How long must a peculiarity like this persist to be addressed a possible condition or disorder? What else is or will go missing from my memory?

When it's time to head home, I decide I need to take some action, to at least tame the swirl of anxiety.

So in the evening, in my moonlit kitchen, I call you and say, "I know this is going to sound crazy and even offensive, but can you tell me your name?"

Because maybe if you tell me your name, you will once again have a name in my thoughts.

There is only silence from you, so I add, "Sorry, somehow, I just can't remember what it is."

"Oh, don't you worry about my name," you answer vaguely. "You know who I am, and that's what matters."

Your words and tone of voice are comforting, but I don't understand why you're reacting this way. Maybe you're trying to be sympathetic, but you seem so unconcerned about the possible implications of this situation. Maybe you don't grasp the potential severity of what's going on.

"Really, it's fine," you add.

"But it's been terribly disconcerting!" I nearly shout into the phone. "I know that I know—or knew your name, but I can never recall what it is. I don't even know what letter it starts with!"

"Well, you're probably just… tired or under a lot of stress," you say simply, seeming a little distracted. "And I'm sure this summer heat isn't helping either. Don't let this bother you. Just relax."

"All right, sure," I reply.

I lean on the counter. Then, not knowing what I can now possibly say to get to you to take this seriously, I say good night.

But you do take this seriously. Aware now the shortcomings of your strategy, you immediately take a more thorough approach.

Hours later, after I'm sound asleep in bed, you let yourself in with the spare key I gave you. Silently and meticulously, you comb from my mind all knowledge that people must have names, eliminating all expectations that you have a name and that I should know it. With that done, I will no longer find it weird that I don't know your name, that you apparently don't have a name. Then you mend the associations you previously severed, re-routing them so that upon seeing you or hearing your voice, emotions and memories will spring to mind; upon recognizing you, the absence of a name will be superseded with familiar feelings and warm recollections.

Finally, to enable me to talk about you with other people normally, you reconnect my knowledge of your name to my unconscious mind, where it will remain out of reach of my consciousness. The result: I will be able to say your name to people and recognize when people refer to you by name; I will also be able to write down and read your name, yet I will have no conscious perception and no conscious memory of it, no awareness that I've used or encountered your name. Like you've engineered some kind of blind spot in my consciousness, all uses of your name made subliminal, effectively invisible and inaudible.

And this works. In the morning, I mentally shrug at your

lack of a name in my memories, uncertain why I was so upset yesterday.

Now, in my mind and in my life, you are simply *you*.

The Importance of Hiding Places

I'm savoring another cool breeze that's meandering through this seaside town, when a wide smile instantly brightens your face into an expression of pure glee. It happens at the edge of my peripheral vision, but it's unmistakable, immediately catching my attention, like someone has just lit a flare.

"Hey, there's a nice little magazine café," you tell me, aiming an index finger at a tiny, rustic storefront just a half block away from the plaza we're loitering in.

And instantly I'm sure I know what you really mean: there's a nice little hiding place, somewhere you can linger without fear of being discovered by people you know. You're always on the lookout for these sorts of places, especially during these late-summer wanderings that we're prone to embark upon every chance we get.

"Don't you think it looks cozy, with an approachably cultured feeling to it?" you ask.

"Definitely," I reply. "It seems like it's got a good balance of simplicity, sophistication and… smallness."

I feel my heart being warmed by our conversation, by this reminder that I'm privy to a secretive part of your life.

Around me, you're comfortable pointing out these places because you know I respect your desire to hide, to seek seclusion. You know I won't tell others about places like this and won't come looking for you either. Unless there's something urgent. Because I know you need these places.

But what I don't know is exactly why you need these places, who you're actually, ultimately hiding from. I've simply concluded that your stints of sequestration are intended to minimize your contact with friends, co-workers, former classmates and neighbors—people whose company you can only handle in limited amounts. Which is true. But an oversimplification.

The crucial piece of information I'm missing is this: If you're around certain people for too long or see them too often, certain selves of yours are bound to show up. They descend upon these social situations as if they've homed in on the scent of clashing political perspectives (no matter how unwitting or minor), or disagreeable opinions on lifestyle choices, or boredom, or condescension.

One of these selves has a habit of barging in and arguing vehemently; you've become all too familiar with him and his outbursts over numerous years. Then there's your timekeeper self who almost always arrives on the scene if some idle chitchat goes on for longer than a few minutes; she impatiently yet discreetly reminds you to be conscious of the time, insistently prods you to check your watch and pays close attention to the conversation with the aim of determining an opportunity to end it. And recently, a newcomer has started appearing during meetings at work, manifesting her superiority complex in condescending and dismissive remarks; she's slowly cropping up more and more outside the office.

Oblivious to all this, I see the café as an escape not from selves but from others. With me, you're comfortable pointing out and talking about these places because I don't know these selves and they could never find you through me.

"Let's go in and take a look around," you suggest merrily, eyes gleaming.

"Okay, I could do with a root beer or something," I answer.

You nod and set off for the café with springy strides. I follow after you.

"Think we'll find some interesting, obscure magazines in there?" you ask.

"There should at least be a good sampling of regional ones," I say. "And maybe among the staff favorites, there'll be some delightful, little-known gems."

"Yeah, it'll be fun to see what their taste is like here."

As we near the café, I peer through its big wood-framed, grey-tinted glass window just beside the matching door. Inside is a self-consistent little world of snugly arranged minimalist furniture and an invitingly colorful assortment of magazines laid out upon bamboo stands. A visceral certainty coalesces in me. I know this is exactly the kind of hideout you could spend hours on end in. Even if I don't know the precise reasons why, I know you'll be coming back here. Frequently.

Caretaking

On your way to the Compulsory Education Through Rote Memorization conference, you leave your imagination in my care so there's no danger he will distract you—or worse, run wild in the company of your colleagues. I don't agree with how you address your concerns, but I understand them. When we were growing up, his vitality used to get you in trouble during class, and ever since, you've been wary of where you take him and where you let him roam. When experiences like this happen at such a tender age, they can cling to the psyche, encumbering it, hindering it from the exercise of better judgment.

I squint as the three of us stand on the strip of cracked sidewalk just outside my apartment building's entrance. The afternoon sky is a beautiful but uncomfortably brilliant shade of blue, fitting for this change of custody.

As always, you've got a tight hold on the leash attached to his collar. He slouches, appearing restlessly patient; even with his drooping posture, his extraordinary stature and vigor are evident, as if he could rise at any moment and instantly transform his latent energy into colorful, even overwhelming dynamism.

"Remember to take him out window-shopping, stargazing and all that so he can get some nourishment and exercise," you tell me.

I nod and reply, "Yeah, I was thinking we could go to that art café with the open mic—"

"*Only* if you're careful!" you're quick to stipulate. "That place can be overstimulating for him with all that exuberance and *poetry*. Take the muzzle if you go. Just in case."

"Well, all right, if you insist," I murmur.

"I don't want him to get too excited. He might bother people or cause me trouble later. Overstimulation can make him really playful or agitated, and that would take up a lot of my attention. To the point where he'll keep me up at night or keep me from getting work done. I don't have the time to engage— *indulge* him in that state."

Maybe you should make the time, I want to say, but this is of course no time to get into all that again.

"Okay. If we go, we won't stay long," I say instead.

"Sounds good," you reply.

You turn to your companion, peer deep into his perceptive eyes and say, "I'll see you soon, darling. *Behave yourself!*"

You hand over the end of the leash to me, and this mighty animal turns towards me, regarding me eagerly with the bright gaze I've come to know so well. Then you hand me the other leashes. First, the very short one with a choker, the one you got when he had that growth spurt and you became afraid that he might become so powerful that you'd get utterly carried away if he ever became hyperactive, that he might lash out at others with incisive sarcasm and satire. Then the slightly longer leash for proper social circumstances and, of course, the muzzle. I doubt I'll need them, but I know you'll make a fuss if I don't take them.

"That should do it. You already have everything else he'll need," you say.

"Right," I confirm, in place of what I really want to say: *of course I do.*

You nod, take one more look at your longtime companion and hug me, because you never like saying *goodbye*.

I watch you head down the block, your departure made especially vivid by the brilliant June sunlight.

Then I go inside and close the door behind me.

I walk up the airy, quiet, storied stairwell, loosely holding the leash, feeling no need to grasp it firmly. There's not much damage he can cause here even if he wanted to, and I've never really minded chasing (or even struggling to keep up with) your imagination. With springy steps, he ascends alongside me.

A few minutes later, we're in my apartment, and after I've shut the door, I remove the leash from your imagination's collar. It isn't long before he sniffs out my imagination, who has been hiding in eager anticipation of this company.

Tomorrow, I'll borrow Yuuka's car, and we'll go out to the northern hills where there are no leash laws.

What We Have in Common

Lately, you've been hogging our shared taste in music, keeping from me our appreciation of this art form. I haven't used it for over a week now, and consequently

- I have to abandon my plans to pick out songs for Xire's birthday and must instead bake her cookies;
- I'm left utterly unable to enjoy (or even be disappointed by) that impromptu visit to the jazz lounge with Zona a few days ago (and while I could discern that the vibraphonist played with exceptional skill and the vocalist expertly modulated her smooth, deep voice, without the taste, I couldn't grasp that je ne sais quoi music has as a richly unified experience);
- I can't soothe my mind after a long day of metaphor building or ease my socioenviropolitical anxieties with zonkoriaphone sonatas or Cerulean Ice Field 53 and their exuberant clarinet solos;
- when asked for musical recommendations, I resort to mining my memories for recommendations I've made before, those given to other people with similar tastes.

And even though my turn with our taste is now long overdue, you show no signs of turning over the taste to me. So this afternoon as we're walking along the horizon, I do what I've rarely had to: ask you for it.

"Yeah, I'm really sorry I've had it for so long," you tell me as we pass by the vanishing point. "I've been meaning to give it to you for a while."

Briefly, I wonder if I should demand the explanation you

don't (but really should) offer me, but I'm afraid the matter will get more complicated or frustrating or sensitive if I do.

"Okay," I simply reply.

"I'll get it to you soon," you assure me.

But you don't. Or you had another time frame in mind for "soon."

Days go by and music remains psychologically vapid, inaccessible to me on intuitive and emotional levels. I yearn for music to fill my ears, mind and life with the radiance it so often has. Even though I don't know exactly what it is I'm craving, I do know that my days are emptier without it.

The continuation of this deprivation of musical discernment eventually pushes me to immerse myself in something I have my own taste in: data visualization. So I visit the library to look at their new chart acquisitions.

When my path to the infographics section takes me by the listening rooms, my pace slows as my habit of glancing into them is triggered. In the first room, a man and a young girl sit at the room's little desk with a couple pop albums in front of them. They seem to be singing along to the song playing on the room's stereo system. I wonder if this is a father-daughter, cost-conscious DIY karaoke session. In the second room, there's an assortment of familiar recordings stacked on its desk. Among the selections are several of your favorites: Nomari's Concerto Z in G minor for ice cream trumpet, "Epiphanal Sunset Drive" by Wendilia Rialsi, *Indiscriminate Karaokables*. Then one of mine: "Love Traffic Jam on Life's Highway" by FJ Trítrí.

At first, I dismiss it as mere coincidence—a chance encounter with someone sampling music that we enjoy.

Then I recognize the lyrics leaking out the slightly ajar door, and I'm instantly in the thrall of a close relative of déjà vu. My eyes fixate on the guy sitting at the desk as he nods his head to the denouement song from the *Loud Thinkers Have No Secrets* soundtrack as it plays on the room's speakers. It feels not like I've seen this before but like there's an intimate atmosphere here that shouldn't exist with a complete stranger. The album playing is too obscure, the musical selections gathered before him too eclectic. It's all so improbable and uncanny.

And it hits me like a puff of air in the eye during an optometry examination. It's not serendipity that accounts for this. It's taste. Our taste.

So *this* is what's happened to it. You've shared it with someone else, or more like loaned it to him indefinitely. I'm filled with the desire to reclaim it right here and now, but it's a library, and I don't want to cause a scene.

"He's really benefitted from good taste in music," you tell me the following day, as we linger on the horizon in post-confrontation awkwardness.

Then get him to cultivate his own, I almost fling at you, but my better judgment stops me, and a split second later, I understand why as my conscious mind grasps what my unconscious one was able to and has now handed off: the implications of this imperative could be severe. You might take this as a cue to cultivate your own taste by sundering the one we've shared and taking the parts you really like—or by leaving it in its entirety with me then growing an entirely new sensibility in music for yourself. Either would sever this connection we've had since high school.

"You should have asked me," I say instead.

"I know," you answer distantly.

"I don't want to be mean, but I really don't want to share this with anyone else," I tell you with a calmness that surprises me. "Maybe occasionally is okay, but I need our taste in music to stay with us. Because otherwise it'll lose its specialness. It's ours, one of the things that's just between us, that we've worked on and enjoyed together. And that's what I need."

You sigh heavily.

"I feel similarly, I truly do," you tell me. "But sometimes I really, really want to share it with someone I've met. Someone whose thoughts would be expanded and even illuminated by the music we've come to love through our taste."

"Yeah, I get that. We wouldn't have our taste if it weren't for all the people who shared theirs with us. But it's actually that kind of sharing that can be the most helpful. We were granted a vital degree of guided exposure that piqued our curiosity and allowed for ample exploration."

We're both silent for a moment, while you consider what I've said.

"Of course, you're right. I got carried away," you tell me. "I wanted him to experience all the amazing music we love with a seasoned sense of appreciation. So he could get right to the stunning idiosyncrasies and beautiful nuance. That was selfish of me. I was impatient."

"Well, it's great you met someone you want to share so much with," I tell you, trying not to sound jealous.

Saying these words, I feel like I'm giving up, but on what I'm not sure. Then my heart becomes tinged with the ache I now realize I've been blockading since seeing him with our taste.

You smile faintly, almost awkwardly.

Then I know exactly where we have to go this evening, the kind of musical atmosphere we need. The insight surprises and delights me, then a moment later saddens me.

Truncated Days

In a sudden blur of goodbyes and well wishing, she leaves, unwittingly taking with her my ability to perceive tomorrow. Alternately appalled by her abrupt departure and preoccupied by projects at work, I don't notice what I'm missing. Until a few days later, when my wall calendar in the kitchen looks eerily odd.

While waiting for my morning coffee to finish brewing, I look at that familiar grid of days, and all the squares after today's fail to mean anything. They don't seem to correspond to anything. It's like looking into someone's living room from their dining room, only to see a blank room or no room at all. I know there should be something beyond today, but it feels like there's nothing.

Left with only awareness of an ever-ongoing today and the past expanding in its wake, I inhabit a constrained temporality. Work becomes just a steady stream of tasks across a continuous workday, home life simply the chores and cooking and relaxation that I undertake as circumstances demand.

It's not so bad. My curtailed sense of time hasn't yet caused any serious issues. Though I do miss being able to plan ahead and look forward to things. Some nights, I go to sleep with the hope that when I wake up, I'll be able to discern tomorrow, even for just a moment—a fleeting comprehension of tomorrow would be a wondrous necessity and crucial luxury now. The vivid and lengthy past can feel excruciatingly unbalanced by the imperceptible future, which even when it was indistinct, had been unmistakably apparent before her departure.

"I wish I could lend you mine," you say as we sit on the

horizon where indigo sands and chartreuse clouds touch each other and us. "There are times when I don't like to be cognizant of tomorrow. But you know how personal the perception of time is to me, and I'm not ready to…"

As your voice trails off, I quickly reply, "I completely understand. Don't worry about it. I don't want you to feel any pressure to do something you're not comfortable with."

"At least you can still perceive the boundaries of yourself," you offer.

"That's true," I say, considering how she could have deprived me of that too, leaving me to blur into the world.

I don't know how you do it.

Superfluous Sentiments

There it is outside the door to my apartment when I get home. More unnecessary sympathy from you, wrapped up neatly in a furoshiki as usual—so I'll have to see you at some point to return the elegant cloth wrapping, at which time you can assess my situation, indirectly by inference and intuition.

I sigh heavily and reach down to pick up the bundle of unwanted commiseration. For its size, it has considerable heft and warmth, making me feel guilty about the annoyance I feel towards you. For a moment. Then I unapologetically reclaim my stance that these emotions of yours are more imposition than assistance. With the sympathy tucked under my left arm, I unlock the door with my right hand and head inside.

I know you mean well, so I've accepted your feelings with appreciation, but it can't go on like this. I thought you'd stop after the fourth or fifth satin-swaddled offering of sympathy, but now I'm holding the *ninth*, and there's no indication that this is the last. By continuing to give me sympathy I don't need, you're making me feel like I'm hopelessly pitiful. And this is straining our relationship.

So despite being worn out, alacrity eroded away by another day of incessant streams of data, I decide to stop by your place tonight.

Mere moments after I've rung the doorbell, you're standing in the doorway, giving me an extra-affectionate smile that feels almost condescending.

"Thanks for the sympathy," I begin, forcing myself to get to the point. "But it's not what I need right now."

I hold the furoshiki-swathed feelings out towards you. Your smile rapidly fades.

"It's the only thing I can give you," you tell me.

Your arms stay at your sides, leaving mine to remain outstretched. I'm surprised by how obvious you make your reluctance to take back your emotions.

"That's because of your perceptions of me. If you can only see me as needing sympathy, that's all you'll feel you can give me."

"Then tell me what you need. Based on what you're saying, I'm not good at figuring that out."

"Just try something. Anything," I encourage.

"What if it's something that bothers you?"

"I'll tell you, and we'll try something else."

"Well, how about some tea?"

"Sure, that sounds nice."

You smile just a little and step aside, welcoming me in with a wave of your hand.

Emotional Engineering

Though it constitutes a breach of our friendship, I take it upon myself to change your mind and reconfigure your reactive tendencies while you're taking an afternoon nap. Just a simple adjustment to bias anger over sadness, one that leaves intact what you'll react to and how frequently. I make sure to keep the triggering threshold high. You didn't cry over spilt milk, and now you won't get enraged over it, so to speak. No sense in you getting incensed about petty matters.

Though this transgression is performed on the spur of the moment, your propensity to respond with sadness has long ruled your life, and its reign has left you disadvantaged—yielding inaction rather than rousing you into action.

Now, the hegemony of dejection is at last broken, and a shift in your behavior is immediately noticeable. Instead of becoming despondent when faced with poor treatment and disappointing conduct, you are riled into ranting and rebuking. You upbraid subordinates for shoddy work on projects you've tasked them with. When you get only mediocre rest, you don't hesitate to take your displeasure to the Sleep Center manager, who promptly gives you three credits. You become outraged on Xire's behalf and lash out against budget cuts to the seaweed farm; this proves instrumental in getting the local aquaculture critics to relent.

With your new temperament serving you well, I delight in your new ire-sparked assertiveness. Until I hear that you've taken to burning bridges, setting ablaze once-amiable connections between you and your peers, torching them with fierce, caustic words when disagreements become disagreeable, then inflammatory. Clashing principles and incongruous values incite your ire, leading you to irrevocably sever ties. Initially, I'm alarmed, but upon further consideration I relax into thinking, "What's the harm in the fiery reshaping your social landscape?" These people would be dealing you despair if I hadn't redirected your emotional response. Better to cut them loose.

But suddenly a spat between you and Murna (your closest academic partner of all people!) blows up into a bitter falling out. And I begin to fret. Struggling to figure out what's happened, how events could take this ugly turn, I mull over several possibilities. The most probable explanation is that Murna has a low-threshold temper that, once agitated, is not easily quelled, and this might have locked the two of you in a disastrous positive feedback loop of escalating arguing. If so, then fault for this interpersonal strife is not primarily yours, and therefore not mine either. Asking around discreetly, I gather evidence to support or overturn the interpretation I've arrived at; mutual acquaintances tell me that Murna has a bit of an aggressively self-righteous streak. So she must've been fanning some flames, causing that particular bridge to blaze.

Then, just as I'm getting a handle on understanding what happened with Murna, further friction erupts. This time with your sister. A tiff over the purchase of her latest status symbol explodes into a drawn-out dispute over familial responsibilities. Apparently, your one and only sibling bought an ornamental designer purse while merely spectating as one of your cousins languishes in the thrall of a high-interest loan.

Over morning coffee in the breakfast garden, you describe what happened, rancor suffusing your voice.

"She just doesn't understand that bonds among relatives shouldn't be purely emotional," you conclude with marked irritation. "I've had enough of her for a while."

And while this behavior of hers isn't entirely new, this behavior of yours towards her is. Until now, you've been sympathetic and patient with her priorities, which sometimes verge on or even venture into excessive and nonsensical self-indulgence. The shift in her sibling dynamics nonplusses me, and I'm left merely murmuring vague agreement with her sentiments.

Several hours later, I suddenly find myself confronted by the unavoidable conclusion that I've precipitated unprecedented problems in your relationships. Frantic, I drop everything I'm doing and go to Xire's studio. We stand in the kitchenette where Xire has been washing dishes after her late lunch, and I tell her everything.

"You did *what*?" Xire exclaims.

"I re-routed the—"

"I know what you did. But I can't believe you took such a liberty," she says. "Everything about his recent behavior makes sense now."

"Really?"

Xire exhales sharply.

"Anger is different from sadness. You've completely overlooked the reinforcing loop that lowers the perturbation threshold," she informs me. "The angrier you are, the easier it is to become angrier. Any residual anger in him is going to make him more prone to becoming angry."

"I didn't think the anger would persist long enough to lower the threshold."

"Yeah, I can see how you went wrong here. He didn't really show his anger. He could remain angry for a while, and you'd never know it."

This eases my guilt a little. This point in the discussion is the closest to sympathy I'll get from Xire. It prompts me to move on with business.

"So what should I—what can be done about it? Redirect the reactive tendencies again?"

"Yes, but it's going to be more difficult this time. We have to change the reactive threshold *and* deal with the buildup of anger."

"So I should go get a whole lot of anger neutralizers?"

"No, that's going to be emotionally confounding in high doses. I think our best bet is to increase the decay coefficient for anger to shorten the half-life and thus the cooling-off period. This should bring down the amount of lingering anger and keep the threshold from falling again."

Over the next two hours, we work out the details of this plan. At Xire's worktable, we make the laborious calculations, the kind of computations I should have undertaken when first tampering with your emotional constitution.

When the numbers look good, handsomely holding up under our careful triple-checking, Xire and I simply nod to each other. The up and down motions of her head are my cue to find you and bring you in for this recalibration. And the intensity of her eyes tells me never to undertake such a surreptitious behavioral modification again.

I should be exhausted from all the intellectual exertion, but I am oddly worked up, emboldened by a new sense of agency and responsibility. I walk outside with energetic, resolute strides, ready to right my blunder.

Aesthetics of the Psyche

When I come back from the kitchen, I find that, alarmingly, you've happened upon my cache of metaphysical erotica. Seated cross-legged on the carpet, you've got the bulk of it spread out in front of you: magazines of the psyche laid bare, books full of charming personalities with stunningly well-proportioned characteristics and cute idiosyncrasies, videos of utterly brilliant minds unencumbered by neuroses, issues of identity or even doubt, engaging in the vigorous, uninhibited (and in some cases explicit) exchange of wondrous, engrossing ideas.

Stopped in my tracks mere steps from you, I just stare at this scene before me, heart pounding.

Until you turn to me and say, "You like this kind of thing?" with a tone that smears together confusion and accusation.

With my mind reeling in this strange turn of events, I say idiotically, "Doesn't everyone?"

"No, not *everyone*," you say fiercely.

I sit down on the floor near you, keeping my distance from the items upsetting you.

"But it's harmless," I somehow tell you. "I just indulge in it occasionally. And it's nothing like the hardcore stuff so many other people are into."

You turn your body so that we're facing each other, your back to my exposed collection of exposed psyches. Our eyes lock in the wreckage of a collision between our gazes.

"But this still promulgates a psychological paradigm that's exaggerated, not to mention narrow," you tell me with such directness it feels as if you've just used telepathy.

"We all know that it's just a bridge to a realm of utter fantasy," I rebut.

"Yes, but that realm still influences this realm. Don't tell me this stuff doesn't sway your feelings about who I am and could be—about how you or I interact with people or how we could interact with them."

"Okay, probably it affects me on an unconscious level," I admit. "But I can still make conscious choices about how I perceive and interact with you or anyone."

"So ignoring for a moment that much of cognition is unconscious, I have a hard time believing that your conscious thoughts about people are completely void of erotic elements. Can you honestly say that you don't harbor kinky conscious ideas about people you know?"

"No, I can't. But can you? And the occasional odd daydream, whether influenced by this stuff or not—I really think that's usually quite harmless."

Then, attempting to shift perspectives, I ask, "And really, isn't this a question of personal freedoms? It sounds like you're taking issue with the extent to which my right to indulge in psychological fantasies imposes upon your right to be accepted as who you are and not compared to some fictitious ideal. Doesn't this kind of tension happen all the time? I mean, some guy might be totally fascinated by women with big egos, but as long as he makes an effort to not be discriminatory in his interaction with women of varying ego sizes, doesn't he have the right to have and express—appropriately—his big ego fetish?"

"But it's more complicated than that," you exclaim, irate now. "By exercising your personal freedom, you are supporting an entire industry and culture of psychological erotica," you rail, voice rising as you shake your open arms as if to indicate how pervasive the industry and its nefarious influences are. "An industry which is only concerned with matters of personal freedoms and the exercise of one's volition to the extent that they can be exploited."

I'm about to take on this whole new dimension of the issue you've introduced, when you come at me again with, "And don't tell me this can be resolved by conscious consumption. You know that's intractably idealistic."

"All right, the commercial aspect is another touchy facet of the whole thing," I concede, nodding. "I acknowledge there is an industry that is exploitative, even manipulative, but then there's an artistic culture and community as well. I mean, isn't part of art to express conceptions of beauty, perfection and the fantastic?"

"The artistic and commercial often aren't cleanly separable."

You reach behind you and grab one of my little indulgences then hold it up before you. I know it well. It's a graphic novel that starts off with a precocious prodigy bumbling into the wrong persona changing room during a conference and in so doing, walks in on a speaker in the midst of doffing her charismatic stage personality, her gorgeously fit mind of shapely wisdom and supple, fragrant empathy fully exposed. Admittedly it's a weak premise by which to get the characters together, and of course, vigorous intellectual discourse ensues. Endearing idealism and authentic values exuberantly entwine with fluid harmony, unstifled by shame, doubt present only in their sensitivity toward each other.

You shake this book at me and demand, "Is this artistic expression or a manufactured product?"

If that's going to be your stance, that we can't talk about art and commerce as anything but intertwined, then all I can say is, "Well, when we become a more ethically capitalistic society and better understand how responsibility depends upon both conscious and unconscious aspects of our minds, maybe then there will be a satisfactory solution to this."

"And in the meantime?" you press me.

I take a deep breath, needing it, keenly certain that you will hold me to my answer. I struggle to give you an answer that I won't regret.

"I'll enjoy what I've got here but try not to buy any more," I decide.

"Okay," you reply with vague satisfaction.

After a moment of silence, you muse aloud, "Maybe if our culture more readily embraced ways to celebrate the naked psyche and its erotic qualities openly and holistically…"

Your voice trails off, and I wonder if this is an invitation to complete the counterfactual you've begun constructing. I'm compelled to think that an answer can be found, at least in part, within the fiction your back is turned to. But there's no way I'm going to mention this to you any time soon.

Unguarded Glances

Lately, I find that I'm not getting the visual information I should be from glances and glimpses. When I quickly look at someone or something, I'll identify the details I want to discern from that brief act of perception, but then I'll wind up completely forgetting what those details were. As if the bit of knowledge I've distilled from the fleeting moment of visual contact were volatile, evaporating quickly from my mind. Like a peek I've just taken hadn't been taken at all.

This leaves me having to attempt another gander or abandon my visual curiosity if the brief window for discreet visual encounters has closed.

In the past week or so, I've done both many times.

Last night, when we were out having dinner with friends, I had a bit of a close call. You proposed we all take a trip together to your favorite hot-spring inn up north later in the month. While Risa—once again the busiest of us all with her sprawling community ties—was checking her schedule, I furtively looked at the calendar she had pulled out of her bag, curious what events and rendezvouses she had coming up. I spotted a couple intriguing engagements and retracted my gaze. But a moment later, I had utterly no idea what I had surreptitiously visually gleaned from her calendar. A dinner date? A deadline? Delivery of an ultimatum?

My gaze went in for another glimpse, but then Risa's eyes rose suddenly and would surely have met mine if I hadn't long ago cultivated the reflex to roll (seemingly in boredom) at the prospect of incriminating eye contact.

And it worked.

Risa simply said, "Okay, towards the end of the month, I don't have too much going on at the moment."

My heart hammered as she folded up her little calendar. Though I have confidence in this ocular maneuver, its execution still unnerves me.

"Great, let's start making plans soon then," you replied, smiling.

"Sounds good," I said distractedly, wondering what I had seen but could no longer make sense of.

Then there was that visit to that chronography studio a few days ago. Xire had invited a few of us to meet a chronographer she had recently started working with. During our short tour of his workspace, I split my attention as inconspicuously as I could between the objects around us and our host as he explained the setup and uses of the various studio areas. I visually explored as much as I could, my gaze rapidly roving the kitchen table, darting to and fro over schematics pinned up on bulletin boards. I stayed towards the back of the group so there would be little danger of drawing attention to the exploration my eyes undertook. Bringing up the rear also made it possible for me to loiter for just a moment in the rooms we moved swiftly through.

I took every opportunity to get glimpses of in-progress chronographs on drafting tables, the faces of people in framed photographs occupying corners of desktops, some titles of books stacked on bookshelves, the typed and handwritten return addresses on envelopes scattered upon a coffee table and decorative flourishes on walls and countertops. But despite being afforded these chances for glances, I found that I often needed to get a second visual helping of the addresses, the faces in black-and-white exuberance on the study desk, miscellaneous knickknacks from cultures I'm not familiar with. Several times, I couldn't get that additional serving because the chronographer was looking in my direction or the rest of our group had entered the next room, and I had exhausted the ephemeral duration in which I could dawdle discreetly. And the disappointment of having nothing to mentally savor or digest hung over me until the next appetizing morsel presented itself.

Especially puzzling was that girl last week, the one who was floating about the idea gallery with an air of autumn nostalgia. Intrigued, I took whatever chances I was afforded to rapidly make observations of her, but I was left with far fewer impressions of her than expected. Despite the variety of tidbits I snapped up with my eyes—her posture, facial expressions, movements—I was missing the characteristics I thought I'd easily collect with each visual plucking, like listless distraction, taste in ideas, subdued thoughtfulness, literary disposition or curiosity in the existential. Those qualities had to be picked up with additional opportunities I lacked the patience to wait for. Frustrated by my inability to acquire enough visual data to form a rough, tentative idea of her demeanor, I gave up and turned my attentions upon the new conceptual work in the gallery. Maybe she had really good mystique.

Even during leisurely moments, the confounding ineffectiveness of my once-reliable glancing practices crops up. That happened again just earlier today, while we were enjoying small bowls of soup in the cozy bistro beside the central train station. I watched the passersby outside, only to become annoyed, then unsettled that I was unable to remember what each looked like once they had moved out of the frame of the large glass window before us. You sat to my right at the counter, seemingly preoccupied by your soup, uninterested in the people walking about the street.

Feeling that I need to figure out what's going on, I give this matter a good long think this afternoon while sipping coffee in the small coffeehouse by the lake. I do some tests, shifting my eyes quickly—from the barista to patrons at other tables to the drinks menu above the percolators behind the cashier—trying to gauge how much I retain from the briefest glimpses. Strangely, these glances feel completely normal; I can remember the detail or two I find interesting in each cursory visual episode, and my mind readily forms impressions from those details. The man at the corner table reading a novel as if to distract himself from his own life. The barista's intensely directed gaze as she operates the espresso machine indicating a keen focus on process. The weekly special of dark roast drip coffee brewed with a splash of jasmine tea, a rather curious combination of caffeine-bearing plants.

So what's different between this bout of glancing and the times when glancing is utterly ineffectual? Could it be that I'm being more deliberate right now? Possible, but I feel I've been rather intentional when looking at other people, objects and situations that pique my attention. What about the circumstances? It's pretty relaxed here; could it be that in places with more bustle, I'm more prone to distraction—to shallower consideration of the glimpses I've taken?

Then, after working through a number of such questions, the pattern presents itself: glances are uninformative only when you are around, and then everything becomes clear.

"You're stealing glances off me, aren't you?"

This is the first thing I say to you the next day, when we meet in the woods for our weekly forest therapy session.

"Well, yes," you admit.

"Why?" I ask, appalled that you'd take advantage of how open-minded I am around you, that you'd just reach over and appropriate my perceptions.

"They're so interesting, and you do it so stealthily," you answer with respectable honesty. "I couldn't help myself."

"I see," I murmur, considering your explanation.

"I didn't mean to keep taking them from you, but once I'd done it a couple times, I couldn't fight the temptation when it flared up," you say, genuinely apologetic. "You know how bad I am at people watching and stuff like that. People quickly sense that I'm looking at them or their things and look back at me."

"Yeah, your gaze lingers too long, among other things," I reply.

"Well, yeah… *exactly.* And you make it look so effortless."

Your words make me less miffed with your recent pilferings.

"It took a while to develop all this observational surreptitiousness. You should keep working at it," I tell you, as encouragement, though I end up sounding defensive.

"But it's embarrassing to get caught!"

"You can't learn to ski if you're afraid to fall," I remind you.

"Oh, *all right,*" you concede.

Then it seems we're ready to move on from all this. And we do so with a moment of quiet communion with nature, becoming entranced by the lushness of oak leaves all about us here.

It compels me to remark, "But, you know, it does help to have a ski instructor."

You perk up and stare at me to make sure you've drawn the right inference.

The wind jostles the branches above us.

A Cold Heart Is An Orderly Heart

"What's with the ice pack?" you ask, pointing at the little plastic bag full of ice cubes strapped to my chest.

"It's to keep my heart frozen," I explain.

"Why? That's rather inconsiderate of you to be so deliberately cold-hearted."

"Yes, but it keeps my heart in orderly form with all the feelings locked in place—no sudden rearrangements, no surprising recombinations, no unwanted shiftings."

"That's really boring too."

"Perhaps, but very manageable, far more tractable than before, you know—"

And before I know it, you curtail my elaboration by launching your fist at my chest, the force it deals crunching the ice, propagating through the crushed cubes to shatter my heart and knock the wind out of me.

"Well, now you'll have to let it all melt and coalesce back together," you say with satisfaction as I gasp for breath.

After a moment, you add, "You'll thank me later, I'm sure."

Diet

As we loiter in the rehearsal room, while the rest of the band is out getting break-time snacks, you sense that I'm about to make some friendly comments about your exceptional xylophone work.

"*Remember*, no compliments while I'm on this ego-slimming regimen," you instruct.

Because you're on a new ego diet. Because you're concerned that your ego is too large and has only been getting larger. But while ego obesity is one of the most troubling epidemics of our times, your ego is far from being unhealthily large.

I sit down in the chair next to yours and ask you, "What if I feel compelled to express some appreciation?"

You cross your arms before answering, "If you must, just give me a little. If it's too much, I'll probably end up throwing it back at you or just neglecting it and letting it go to waste. Which reminds me, be critical of me whenever possible."

"That seems kind of harsh," I remark. "Are you sure you're going to get enough encouragement and positive attention? I don't want to see your psyche all emaciated by the month's end."

"I don't need that much, and I've got a lot of pride. That will keep me going for a while."

"A lot?" I echo incredulously. "If you've got a lot, then I'm in more need of a diet than you are."

"Maybe you are," you hurl back at me. "The way you indulge in the admiration Risa loves to feed you and your frequent cravings for praise, those can only be enlarging your ego."

"Everyone needs some genuine appreciation," I generalize, defensive, irked by your words.

"You make 'need' look like the rest of us are attention-starved."

"The way you're going, you will be," I snap.

"We could all benefit from lifestyles that are less emotionally opulent."

"Well, I feel like I'm getting a healthy amount, and I like the proportions of my psyche."

"Of course you do. It would hurt too much to realize that you're far from ideal."

"Whose ideal?" I demand. "Perfectionists obsessed with the art of selflessness?"

You shake your head.

"An ideal that's grown out of credible research showing that ego reduction can lead to increased quality of consciousness," you say with calm confidence. "Recent studies strongly suggest that we need to undergo a paradigm shift that begins with realizing that what appears to be emotional sparsity is actually plenitude—a realization that can free us from the psychological cravings that create, sustain and exacerbate huge egos."

This prods me to think that maybe I am clinging to soon-to-be antiquated self care practices, but I still viscerally feel that austere deprivation is too extreme.

"Okay, I haven't kept up with recent metaphysiology studies—I should look into that," I concede. "But does the shift you're talking about have to happen through such drastic measures?"

"It only seems drastic to you because it's trying to resolve an overlooked problem that's already in advanced stages. But when you consider the situation, it becomes clear that the solution isn't so radical. Look at this dispute we're having, for instance."

You pause for a moment, as if letting me see the dispute, as though our contending words are hanging in the air before us.

"It alone is illustrative of the problematic size of your ego. You're insistent that I'm wrong, throwing your ample psychological weight around, and based on what? Research data? No, more like adherence to a lifestyle that's comfortable. See what the ego proportions you like so much are doing to you? Having that kind of heft, you're prone to having its inertia dominate your behavior and prone to having it lean on people you don't agree with through your words."

I'm left unable to rebut what you've said, and quite keenly I feel my psyche sag with a heaviness that I can't help but now find concerning.

Silence engulfs us, until you quietly tell me, "I took it pretty hard too," while placing your hand lightly on my upper arm to offer me what feels like just the right amount of warmth.

Stories Belong to No One

Distractedly, I ooze honey from its dispenser into the mug of morning coffee I just ordered, then head to the end of the counter nestled in the corner of the café. My mind is once again mulling the interpersonal distance that's been between us lately. It's no rift, by no means a chasm tearing the social landscape we inhabit. More of a nebulous, mild alienation that nonchalantly keeps our psyches apart. Like a cold fog that's settled between us, that neither one of us wants to traverse, with enough opacity for us to lose track of each other, to just wander away.

But no matter how I picture this separation, it just doesn't make sense. This remoteness from each other sprung up without warning. There were no indicators that I had offended you or that you needed space to yourself. Or have I missed all the clues? When you receded from me, did all the hints then become impossible to pick up?

I swirl the coffee with a small metal spoon to dissolve the honey. Then, abruptly, the color of the café coffee mug gives everything away. You've slipped up and unwittingly revealed that this is your story.

Though I visit this underground café only occasionally, I come here often enough to have noticed that all the mugs are—were periwinkle. Now the one before me and all those I see around the café on tables and shelves, they're all cornflower blue, one of your all-time favorite colors. So unless they've just recently replaced their mugs (unlikely with the economic climate of our town) this change could mean that you wield far deeper influence than I could ever have imagined.

Flabbergasted, I simply stare at the mug before me on the tabletop, transfixed by its normally innocuous, now-disconcerting hue. This almost insignificant detail casts all I've known into doubt. What's my role? Where's the plot headed? Did you concoct this? Am I supposed to have this existential crisis right this moment as an element of character development?

Uneasily, I begin to sip hot, strong coffee from the piece of incriminating evidence. The thoroughly familiar beverage soothes me enough to let my mind wander back to more mundane matters. I have an ecology design meeting to attend soon, and whether I'm central to the narrative structure or not, I have responsibilities towards my colleagues, whatever kinds of characters they are.

With that in mind, I manage to relax, to carry on as I usually do, as if this were my story.

Strangely enough, the meeting goes smoothly for me despite the implications of the coffee mug. There are lulls in the discussion during which I wonder how the increased distance between us might relate to the revelation in the café, but as my team works through our agenda items, I'm far more engaged in the meeting than I expected I'd be. Maybe that's because glimpsing the true nature of this story and the nature of your role here, that only changes my conception of the circumstances, only alters the world on a philosophical level; the basic structure of this world is still the same as it's always been.

"Hey," Xire says, walking towards me as I gather up my things from the conference table.

"What's up?" I ask her, wondering if she's a main or supporting character; I can't see her as the protagonist.

"I was just about to ask you the same. You have this cloud of preoccupation about you."

I consider mentioning what happened in the café, but this doesn't seem like a good time and place to talk about that. Instead, I offer something comparatively paltry.

"Oh, there's suddenly a lot of distance between myself and someone I've been close with," I tell her. "I'm not sure what to do about it."

"Have you two talked about it?" Xire asks with concerned curiosity.

"No, it's only just happened."

"If you've been close for a while, you should be able to ask this person what's going on, even from outside the usual relationship comfort zones. You might get a terse or vague answer, but at least you'll have some idea of why there's new distance between you two."

"I suppose that's true."

"I think that most of the time, it's better to discuss matters like this, unless someone really doesn't want to talk about what's going on. And even then, it's better to find out that they really don't want to talk."

"I like how you dislike ambiguity," I remark.

"There are so many things in this world we can never be sure about, so I like to be sure about the important ones I can be."

It's hard to argue with that.

I compose a short note to you on a scrap origami paper that's thoroughly creased with numerous cycles of folding and unfolding. After I tack this note on the community message board in the lobby of the social center, my gaze wanders the board, searching for items.

With that done, I consider the errands that need doing, but this train of thought doesn't get very far. A heavy fatigue begins to weigh upon me. I've been riding the momentum of the meeting's energy, and now that's all dissipated away, lost to the friction of moving through the world. Instantly it makes complete, persuasive sense to get some rest here.

Trudging upstairs to the sleep room, I long more and more with every step for the nap I've decided to take there. When I lie down, it feels like I've barely managed to get here, to pull the futon Xire, Rika and I share from the storage area and unfold it on an open patch of the tatami floor—feels like I had just enough energy to make it to this point in spacetime, the gateway into a swath of comfortable sleep.

The ensuing slumber, though restful, is riddled with peculiar dreams. While I'm engaged in mundane or extraordinary circumstances, I'll suddenly see you just standing around, watching me.

Toiling deep in a hope mine with a team laboriously extracting the ore of optimism, I move towards a new patch of raw hope embedded in the earth. The beam of my headlamp sweeps across a segment of the mineshaft, suddenly revealing you standing amid the darkness. But after an instant of recognition, I don't give you a second thought, as if you're supposed to be there, supervising the work or observing us to learn the mining practices.

Later, I'm visiting a relative, perhaps an uncle, who is convalescing in a mountainside villa. Out on the patio, his doctor explains to me that he has been suffering from cause blindness but has responded well to treatment. Unable to construe causation, he has been experiencing the world without cause and effect relationships; in that state, the world just happens as isolated, unrelated episodes—past, present and future actions connected only by the flow of time.

"Occasionally, he still has difficulty verbalizing the causal structure of events," the doctor tells me. "Just yesterday, he could not tell us why the curtains in his room opened after he pulled their drawstring. But the fact that he pulled the drawstring to open the curtains, presumably to let in the morning sunlight, indicates that his unconscious grasp of causation is likely normal, at least in that instance."

"And he's expected to make a full recovery?" I ask.

"We have every reason to think so," she assures me. "All the test results are so far excellent."

I nod, my gaze restless, moving across the scene. And there you are, standing at the edge of the patio that overlooks the garden.

Then, while hiking in some hills, letting time dilute the reality of recent events and relationships, I am impatient for the ties of vestigial friendships to dissolve, while trying to savor the tail end of this year's poppy bloom. I pass by ecologists examining indicators of ecosystem health and pass by you too as you stand among them.

Bemused but refreshed, I sit up and rub my eyes. Though the dreams are fading, dimming out of my memory, they are still fresh enough to preoccupy me for a couple minutes. Long enough to know that you were always a pervasive observer in them, a consistent element across disparate settings. This is a realization I can have only now that I've woken up.

Alongside me are a few slumbering townsfolk who must have come in during my nap. As quietly as I can, I put away the futon and head downstairs to check the message board. There's a reply from you scribbled beneath the one I left you: *All right. I've been meaning to talk with you. Greenhouse at 5 p.m.?*

I quickly jot *Yes* beneath your words.

I find you standing by a table crowded with rows of fledgling aloes.

"So, where does this conversation start?" you ask, yet again deferring to me for a point of departure.

"This is your world, isn't it?" I can't stop myself from asking—accusing.

"Well, partially, yes," you reply casually, like I'm just a latecomer to an awareness everyone else has already settled into.

Taken aback by your treatment of the situation, I'm only further bewildered, only able to ask, "What do you mean?"

"This world is what connects us, where our experiences overlap as authors, characters and audience. Sure, it's easier to think of it as someone's story, but that's a drastic over-simplification."

"So what are you saying? That this story is everyone's and no one's?"

"*Relax*," you urge. "Everything's been fine so far—why blow this out of proportion?"

"But who's the narrator? You, me—someone else entirely? Is that person also the protagonist?"

"Look, these elements aren't cleanly separable in some cases. The story simply grows, continues to happen. I'm just helping the part I'm embedded in to develop."

"But how am I—how are we supposed to… help the story develop if we don't have clear-cut roles?"

My voice is taut with frustration. Maybe the humid warmth here is compounding the confusion.

"The utility of roles always has a limited range. They're effective guides for behavior in certain situations, but you know that we are much more than the roles we've taken on. On the institute campus, you might be largely regarded as an ecological engineer, but even then you aren't just an expert in configuring ecosystems. And you have an identity that extends beyond your roles."

"Then what gives the story coherence if not consistent roles and perspectives?"

You sigh heavily.

"Don't confuse the structure of your conscious experience with that of stories. In your experience of the world, there's a single, constant perspective that you are directly aware of, that seemingly binds everything together. But the world, of course, isn't just you. Much like the interplay of varied thoughts and feelings gives rise to intricacies of the mind, our world is fluid and in flux. It can't be decomposed into relationships that can be neatly classified like the ones you study—symbiosis, predation, competition and nurturance, those are far more static than our relationships with each other and the story."

"So then the story just is, exists as an ever-dynamic system in which we are elements with changing properties," I interpret.

"Yes, you could say that. To put it simplistically, we are all—to varying degrees—the actors, audience, set designers, stage crew and production managers in the world theater, each of us taking on and passing on these capacities."

"Then in one of these capacities we come in and out of, you changed the color of the underground café mugs," I surmise.

Your face creases with confusion.

"What? No, I didn't change any café mugs. At least not deliberately, not consciously."

Slapped in the face with consternation, I'm stupefied.

Rather than get tangled up trying to unravel what happened with the coffee mugs, I backtrack in the conversation and ask, "Is this common knowledge? That we exist in this state of fluidity? Is it just me who's late to the party?"

"I'm not sure. This is my understanding of our relation to each other and the world we inhabit, and I have confidence in it, but others have probably arrived at different conclusions based on their experiences."

"Then the ultimate nature of everything here could be completely different from what you're saying."

"There's always that possibility, that there is a subtler, stranger structure—one that could completely elude our comprehension, but this is the best human-oriented perspective I've got at the moment."

You've barely finished saying this when your morlorb beeps with an urgent message. You pull the little device from your pocket and glance at the message.

"Sorry, I've got to take care of this, and it'll take a little while. We can talk more about your concerns tomorrow. I know you're going through an overwhelming paradigm shift, but take it easy, and get a good night's rest."

"Okay, yeah, I'll see you tomorrow," I murmur, everything making much less sense now.

You place a hand on my shoulder for a moment, then head down the rows of tables crammed with seedlings.

I walk down the street calmly aglow with twilight, finding myself oddly unnerved by our conversation. I can't say she's overreacting; it's not unreasonable to feel that a particular story is your own, that you are the protagonist. But you can't impose that kind of structure upon this world. You can't fit it to neatly defined rules, notions of what it should be. Stories are interactions, and authorship isn't singular. Though she might be rattled by that, I'm sure that soon she'll become more comfortable with the collaborative creation we're entwined in.

And we were so caught up discussing this that we didn't get to talk about what I've been wanting to tell her. But that can wait until tomorrow.

Externality

Lately, I've begun to feel apprehensive about my romantic future as intimacy-related anxieties slowly crowd my mind. As the days go by, I become increasingly uncertain, even doubtful about my lovability and psychological attractiveness. The insidious transformation is all so distressingly unnerving and unfamiliar. It's so unlike me to spiral into worry of this sort. And I'm ill-equipped to handle the mind-racking inquisition of skewed, romance-centric, folly-and-fault-seeking thoughts. As doubts sap my confidence, I have no testimonials to retort with, no counterexamples pre-articulated, no psychological shelter stockpiled with affirmation to seek refuge in.

Later, as I'm trying to enjoy my customary cup of evening yogurt at my desk tonight, I realize what I'm going through *is* familiar, and it becomes clear what's going on. Outrage supplants the dread of romantic inadequacy and incites me to take the situation head on. I grab the phone and call you.

"Stop projecting your insecurities onto me!" I demand the moment you answer, my words delivered with a force that aspires to expunge the odious self-doubt right here and now.

"What are you talking about? I'm not doing *anything* to you," you tell me.

"I've been plagued by questions of why I'd ever deserve someone's love when you know very well I've long since grappled with those issues during my adolescence."

"Well, *you* know very well that feelings like that can resurge or simply spring up, especially if you met someone really amazing," you counter. "Or could it be that you're feeling guilty about something you were previously unscrupulous about?"

"Nothing remotely like that has happened lately, and this self-deprivation of confidence is precisely the self-esteem issue of yours that keeps cropping up."

"Actually, it hasn't cropped up at all recently."

"That's because you're projecting it all onto me!"

"I can't believe you're so sure of your conclusion! Here I am, my personal issues at last abating, and there you are, starting to doubt your self-worth, so you just assume the two *must be* connected," you rebut, tone becoming self-righteous. "Did you consider any other possibilities at all?"

"Look, let me put it this way: have you done anything constructive with your insecurities?"

"I've been… living my life, letting the world effect positive change upon me."

"Insecurities seldom get taken care of that way. You have to work at it! You've just pushed it all outside yourself, unconsciously apparently."

"You always think life can be explained by the studies and theories you've read or heard about, but sometimes things just happen without easily identifiable causation! Who knows? Maybe I overcame my insecurities in my dreams!"

"Yeah, okay, so I have a bias towards the logical and probable, but what about you, getting all defensive all the time? It's no wonder you've got insecurities—you overcompensate in ways that never resolve them."

"*Defensive?* How else can I respond when *you* call me up and fling at me this unsubstantiated accusation?"

"All right, I'm sorry about that, but I'm frustrated by this motif in your life of dealing with your personal problems by not dealing with them."

"You know what?" you ask, voice rising further. "We're

not having this conversation—not now, not for a while. I was enjoying a nice piece of spinach, tomato quiche, and you, *out of nowhere*, throw your troubles at me, insisting that I'm their source—based on what, a possible correlation?"

"Fine, I might be wrong, but given your track record of—"

"What did I just say? We are *not* talking about this. At least not until some later time."

"All right, yeah, just push me and these matters away."

"Well, after you've shoved them in my face, how do you think I'm going to react? Call me tomorrow, and maybe we'll talk."

"Okay."

We hang up.

If you were projecting your insecurities on me, these words have undoubtedly deflected the projection. Whatever the case, I feel better already.

The Palatability of Pride

I swallow some of your pride, and it is disgusting. The mouthful goes down gritty and thick, gooey and bittersweet in a way nothing should ever be. A rancid, sandy molasses so thoroughly unpalatable, threatening to coat my throat for days to come.

I grimace at the still half-full bottle of the stuff sitting between us on the plaza table that I feel the need to lean heavily upon now. I slump forward. The sun suddenly feels very hot on the back of my neck.

"Dude, I don't know if I can take any more than that," I tell you.

A keen queasiness sets in.

"Yeah, I know it can be intense," you reply sympathetically. "I've had a tough time downing it on my own. So I really appreciate your help. Maybe if you're feeling up to it, you could take another dose later this week."

A breeze that should be refreshing only exacerbates the nascent nausea. The intensification of my already concerning wooziness calls into question my willingness to be part of this endeavor. I want to see what you're capable of with less pride— how much you can learn and grow once pride no longer keeps you obsessed with being right, acting like you know it all. But if this is any indication of the toll to be taken on my physiology, that's a price I'm not willing to pay.

"I don't know," I begin, shaking my head slowly. "That was quite nasty. I'd actually prefer not to do it again."

"Well, I'm sorry you feel that way."

After a moment, you add, "I thought you'd be delighted to

help me out with this."

You look at me with unmitigated directness, as if to peer into my psyche.

"I thought this would become a legendary moment between us, something we'd look back on as a major milestone towards the big time," you tell me, voice rising. "You know how much I could accomplish once this is out of the way. And you'd benefit tremendously. In fact, you already have. The project I let you interview me for, that's just one example."

I'm about to tell you that I was being polite that time, that your participation didn't really contribute as much as I let you convince yourself. And that if anything, I've long supported you in a variety of less obvious, more amorphous ways, like just being around you when you need company.

But we've been through versions of the argument that could be flaring up now, and it won't help to fan those flames yet again. I had hoped that by helping you get rid of some of your pride, we could start getting past this, toward a point where you see feedback not as an attack but a cue to learn and improve. Clearly, we're still far from that.

"I've got to get going," I simply say. I point to the bottle of odious psychological stuff. "This will take some digesting, and I have a lot of work tomorrow."

I expect some snide or reviling remark from you, but you just reply with, "All right. Hope that goes well. I'll call you later."

"Cool," I answer, rising a bit unsteadily from my seat.

It is an unwelcome challenge to negotiate my way through the summertime liveliness of the plaza with my stomach precariously teetering between being slightly unsettled and heaving in frantic rejection of its new contents. But I know the path, so it is only a matter of minding the obstacles.

As I near the monorail station, the discomfort eases up

enough for me to feel a familiar, resolute glow in the pit of my stomach, reminding me that your pride has a good, strong dignity to it.

Dysquietude

The sudden quietness of your thoughts recently unnerves me. The almost complete disappearance of those lively melodies has flattened my perceptions of you—deprived you of the abundant and nuanced depth you've always had. Today, the faintness of your thoughts makes the sculpture forest unusually, uncomfortably loud, muting my own thoughts so that the space between you and me is particularly empty of us, full only of blaring summer sunlight.

It's been increasingly like this since you became a nightmare surrogate.

"I'm going to take away people's nightmares so they can sleep soundly," you proudly proclaimed when you got the job.

Naïvely, I smiled. You've always been adept at handling your own nightmares, so I figured this line of work would suit you well, although I did have some vague misgivings. Those have since transformed into a shadowy dread that seems to be now draped over us.

Now, with our thoughts muffled, there is nothing to keep the din of the world around us at bay. The sculptures closest to us are raucous with their avant-garde geometry. Keenly I feel the compulsion to fill this void between us with some kind of vibrance, but I'm afraid doing so may irritate you, and my heart tinges with a fear that is unfamiliar to me—a fear akin to what a child might feel when shrinking away from the suddenly stern reticence of a parent who has always been verbosely affectionate.

"Let's go this way," you say, voice booming as you point at

.

the path lined by metal mobiles.

"Okay," I agree, hoping that in taking the direction that interests you, your thoughts might grow more audible.

"Xona is going on a short trip to Trunderbluf next week," you tell me almost thunderously as we start walking—our pace sluggish, as if the habitual motions of our legs and feet are barely adequate to propel us through the viscous sunlight we're immersed in.

"Should be nice this time of summer," I remark.

"Yeah," you agree, nodding. "When she told me about her plans for Trunderbluf, I began to think that I'd really like to go there again."

But I can't hear those thoughts of yours, the desire to visit Trunderbluf totally silent.

"Maybe when you've got some vacation time saved up, we could go there together," I venture, hoping your thoughts might resonate with these words.

"Okay, maybe," you answer.

As we continue down what feels like a corridor of vociferously flapping, twirling and wobbling metal parts and their hissing shadows, your thoughts remain hushed, and I become strangely heartened by your words.

Interstices

The gaps in reality are bothering me again. Just this morning I was walking by an empty gravel lot where fissures in the actual revealed the possible, a vibrant community garden—merely the idea of it, the possibility. I started sneezing almost immediately. I walked away hurriedly to avoid any chance of more severe reactions.

Normally, I'd tighten the mind clamp to compress my imagination and hold my thoughts together in a more focused bundle, but out of sheer laziness, I just leave it as it is, despite these gaps grating on my consciousness.

"Want to go cloud shuffling tonight?" you ask this afternoon while we stand in the odorless room, olfaction cleansing after the hours we've spent quality-control testing the latest entries into the scent index.

Fortunately, there are no gaps in the reality around us, as if no possibilities could reside within the space enclosed by the stainless steel walls. Being here is a much-needed respite for my perceptions of scent and possibility.

You prod at my silence by adding, "I hear they're gonna be pretty puffy this evening."

"Naw," I reply, knowing that discomforting discontinuities in reality are bound to come up while cloud shuffling.

"I know you usually like wispies, but fluffies can be delightful too," you add.

"Yeah, usually I'd be up for that, but I'm tired out."

"Bummer. Well, maybe next time."

I'm about to murmur an automatic echoing of "Maybe next time," but then I notice it between us: a gaping rift in reality containing the unfulfilled promise of genuine closeness, the nebulous notion of an authentic relationship.

Despite feeling my stomach turn, I peer into this chasm of possibility. Spurred on by curiosity and vague hope, I reach in, towards what appears to be a moment of meaningful conversation. I get ahold of it quickly, even if clumsily at first. But soon I find that I can't pull this episode of rapport from the realm of potential by myself. I can only extract some of the words—and you seem completely oblivious to my efforts.

"You ever feel surrounded by possibilities… ones you can enact and ones you can't?" I attempt.

"Sometimes," you say as if making an absentminded movement akin to running your hand through your hair or folding your arms across your chest.

"Like you can see the world as it could be?" I try again.

"Sure, doesn't everyone?"

And with that, I let go of the potential conversation, surrendering it to the company of its unrealized kin.

"Well, I should get going," I murmur.

"Okay, I'll see you later then. Let me know if you change your mind about the cloud shuffling."

Turning away from you and the rift between us, I head out of the odorless room.

When I get back, my apartment is riddled with small holes showing myriad domestic possibilities: the formulation of travel plans I've only daydreamed about, now-overdue letters I've been meaning to write, interesting meals I should cook and uncluttered tabletops long strewn with eclectic miscellanea. Full-on queasiness sets in rapidly.

I slump into my armchair. From the heap of magazines on the coffee table before me, I pick up a months-old issue of *The Casual Anthropologist* in hopes of distracting myself. Flipping through the featured article on the little province of Trunderbluf, I find scenes of urban and rural life in which there are no gross discontinuities in reality, where actuality is smoothly maturing out of possibility. A weathered schoolhouse is adorned with new window gardens, wind turbines dot a hillside ascending from fields tended by generations of farmers, treehouses suspended in a lakeside forest are home to engineers, politicians and artists who gather every Wednesday for potluck dinners. There, the possible and the real flow in and out of each other effortlessly, harmoniously. I consider for a moment that these scenes could have been expertly photographed or touched up to give a compelling but false impression. Whatever the case, these magazine images are a stark contrast to what surrounds me.

I'm about to give in and just adjust the mind clamp as I probably should have when this all started. But then faint sounds from behind me pique my attention, like music through a wall that muffles it into a mere murmur of a melody. I turn to face its source, finding this muted song wafting out of a crack in reality between me and my zonkoriaphone case.

My eyes start to sting, as though someone were cutting pungent onions. The song evokes a poignant wistfulness. Squinting, I get up and go over to the case. As my eyes grow blearier, I open up the case and take up the instrument I loved so much as a child.

With the familiar heft of the long-neglected zonkoriaphone upon my hands, I start to draw out the melody from the crevice it lies within, slowly closing this one of reality's many open seams, while blinking out tears that seem to carry away the irritation that then no longer fills my eyes.

Lost in the Moment

You borrow my concentration to finish a project because recently yours has been fragile and is easily broken, and I don't need mine while I'm letting my mind wander these days. Then it disappears—after the project is done, conveniently enough.

When you break the news to me, I exclaim, "*You lost my concentration?*" in a hushed, hissy snarl.

Wrenching my gaze from the eyepieces of the psychoscope I've been peering into, I regard you with panicked dismay. Mine aren't the only eyes on you. My little outburst has piqued the curiosity of others in the lab.

"Yeah, I'm really sorry. I'll get it back," you say, your words tremendously heartfelt.

And while I don't doubt your determination to recover the concentration, I very much doubt the odds of recovery are high, because what is high is the demand for concentration. It is after all one of the most precious resources for transforming ideas into realities. If my concentration has already fallen into someone else's hands, it will almost certainly be kept and used—or sold.

"Well, tell me what happened," I ask, trying to regain some composure.

"Everything was going splendidly. I was cranking along and got all the work done, so I went out for a walk to relax, and when I got back, it was just *gone.*"

"Can you show me where you left it? Where you last had it?" I ask, hoping we'll turn up a clue there.

"Sure. It was just in the studio alcove."

With hurried strides, we head out of the lab and pedal

our bicycles urgently through the dense summer heat, past tall thickets of skeinweed.

We burst into the co-op studio, losing no time getting to your workspace.

"It was just right here," you tell me, pointing to an empty patch of countertop.

And promptly I burst into laughter, to your sheer consternation. My abrupt change in mood starts to unnerve you. You probably think that I've lost my sanity now too.

"And it's still here," I tell you.

"*What?*" you murmur, incredulous and gawking.

"Expand your awareness a little more," I instruct.

And you start to feel it, that air of focused attention, that force permeating the space to gather and direct effort.

"*Man*, what a relief," you blurt, slumping against the wall. "And it's normal for it to be like that?"

"Yup. Concentration becomes really unobtrusive and transparent after a while. Easy to overlook. When you're using it to its fullest, really connected with it and engaged in what you're doing, it just feels like it isn't there—concentration just blends into everything you're doing. Hasn't that happened to you before?"

"Maybe it has, and I mistakenly thought my concentration had dissipated or gotten used up."

"Well, that happens too. I've exhausted my concentration before, but only when I'm using it for long periods of time or doing something really intense. Is that how you usually work? To the point where you're severely depleting your concentration and becoming totally fatigued?"

"That's what I thought I was doing, but I haven't worked to the extent that I'm completely wiped out."

"So you're working, then it seems like you're out of

concentration?"

"That's right. Then later I have to build up more concentration."

"No wonder you have problems maintaining the integrity of your concentration," I reply, knowing full well how newly formed concentration tends to be less robust. "Are you sure you've been running out of concentration all those times? You weren't just overlooking it like you did just now?"

"Now that we've been talking about this, it's very possible that I may have just walked away from my concentration when I thought it was all gone."

"You should try looking for it. You might be able to regain some of your concentration if you've left it in places where no one would end up taking it."

"Right, I'm definitely going to do that as soon as we're done here. Speaking of which, what do we do now? Just wait?"

"Yes. With a little time, concentration becomes less pervasive and reverts to its more compact form," I explain. "The form that you're familiar with, that you'll find yours in if it's still around. It won't take long, so I'll take it from here. You go find your concentration."

You nod and rush out.

I savor the atmosphere, letting it condense my thoughts into coherence and clarity. Among them is the hope that soon I'll feel this around you more often, feel your concentration transforming space, ideas and us.

As the Past Tries to Catch Up
With You: Part I

The moment I've let you in, you frantically tell me, "She's found me," then quickly close the door behind you.

At first, "she" doesn't mean much to me, but a moment later I realize there is only one person you'd talk about with such urgency: your past self.

"What happened?" I ask as you take off your shoes in the little hallway that leads into my living room.

"She just showed up outside my apartment," you tell me, wiping sweat from your brow. "I saw her through the door's peephole, panicked and fled via the fire escape."

"So you're going to hide out here?" I surmise.

"No, no. It's only a matter of time before she figures out you're here too. I need to borrow a bag, some clothes and money. I have to get out of here for a while."

"You're going to just take off?" I ask, not understanding how that's even an option.

"There isn't really much choice."

Your answer feels like a weak placeholder for a cogent explanation that you're unwilling to share or unable to articulate. Then I notice your large hands trembling slightly, and the seriousness of this situation gains palpable clarity in my mind. But questions persist.

"Where do you plan to go? What about your job?"

"I can't tell you anything more. She may try to find me through you," you say hurriedly.

"Why do you need to evade her so desperately? Why is she

coming after you?"

"She wants to remind me of things, get me to finish certain... endeavors that I don't feel are important right now—that I really can't devote my attention to."

"And you can devote attention to running from your past self?"

"Well, yes."

I look at you skeptically.

"Right now, I'm seeking your help and respect, not understanding."

"Those are usually connected."

"Can't trust play a role here?"

"Okay, if you're going to invoke trust, fine, I trust you enough to go with this, but I still have doubts."

"Those will have to wait. I should get going. She might very well be on her way over here right now."

"All right. Take what you need and have a good trip," I tell you.

"Thanks. I hope we'll meet again soon."

I can't help but think you meant that without the "soon"; I know how much you've left behind to get away from your past self before. You head for my bedroom, and I doubt I'll ever see my indigo plaid shirt again.

In the days, then weeks after you've taken off, it just feels like you're once again busy with projects for clients, trapped in a schedule that's packed too tightly for lunch together, a short hike in the hills or an evening concert. But slowly, the reality of your absence solidifies in my mind, turns from nebulous abstraction to visceral certainty, though I'm often distracted from it by work. In attempts to expedite finalizing the key elements of the cognitive antigen library my R&D group is compiling, we've accelerated our design cycles for developing immunogens.

Which means our team has a lot of concept dissection and recombination to churn through. So there's plenty to keep my mind from wondering about you.

When the occasional reminder of you crops up (like yesterday, when someone ordered your favorite at the juice bar), I'll get curious about where you and your past self are. Is she stealthily closing in on you, or have you managed to throw her off track with some clever red herring that sends her in an entirely counterproductive direction? But with no new information since your departure, with nothing to base the formulation of accurate thoughts, any speculation I can attempt is brief and vague. Sure, I could imagine outlandish scenarios of incessant cat-and-mouse maneuvering or your serene seclusion in an idyllic locale, but without a purpose for such hypotheticals, I lack the motivation to imagine them.

Time proceeds as unsteadily as always in sluggish hours, then spurts of days, and the grip of the summer sun upon the landscape eases. The din of buzzing cicadas vanishes from the local soundscape, the lush, high walls of skeinweed starts to wither, and the humidity is no longer irritatingly palpable. When I'm not at work, I become engrossed in novels and dabble in prosumer holography. Sparks of romance flicker, ever rhythmically the lucidity of dreams intensifies then diminishes, conversations flare up, the embers of interest in inconsequential hobbies are buried under newfound artistic indulgences.

Another certainty begins to coalesce, condensing out of possibility's aether with the seasonal changes. I acclimate to the fact that any overlap our lives have had has ebbed to leave us connected only through the past now.

The Company of Your Past Selves

At the far end of the conference table, she throws up her arms in protest, reviled by the briefing slides management has just presented. I roll my eyes. Here we go again.

"Yeah, why don't you just keep diluting the efficacy with more strategy elements that pander to egotism instead of conducting empathic research?"

She yells this emphatically, true to your lofty ideals which were so intense several years ago.

I don't respond. I can't. Not in the middle of the meeting she's criticizing. And she doesn't expect any response. She knows that the most she's going to be here is a commentator, locked out of the arena of docile gladiators lazily swinging shoddy market research easily deflected by shields of cognitive biases.

"And while you're at it, make the point of your proposal even more ambiguous with a few more layers of jargon-laden abstraction."

Her words are flung forcefully, like she's storming the arena to take on all the contenders. But her outburst—visible and audible only to me—is really just another way she takes advantage of her ethereal habitation of my life. Imperceptible to everyone but me, she can appear to cozily curl up in a chair that would otherwise be empty (and still is empty from the perspective of my colleagues) and freely rant, reassuring both of us that she knows best.

Fortunately, she is the only of her kin who routinely comes with me to work and into the city. Though it would be nice to have the companionship and insights of the more optimistic and receptive selves, I don't think I'd be able to handle having an entourage of them. Especially around you. That would be awkward for me and most of them. Probably you too.

You still have no idea that I harbor the selves you once were, to keep them from fading into the invisible past, the vast expanses of undocumented artifacts, vague memories and dissipated emotions. They also keep me company, reminding me how it used to be between us.

When the workday is at last over, she and I ride the train home. Both tired. Me from work and she of corporate inefficiencies. She makes no comments about the presentation she lambasted. That's a pleasant surprise. Her penchant for pontification (and thus polarizing conversations) is one of the main reasons why you are no longer her. I do admire her unswerving dedication to the values she embraces but wish she didn't have to be so outspoken.

"How about picking up some cookies from L'Orfu Bakery on the way home?" she suggests.

"Of course you'd suggest something indulgent when I have precious little willpower to resist it," I reply.

She nods smugly, then with a flick of her wrist tosses back the long hair that you haven't had since you were her.

Two stations and a few blocks later, we're striding into her favorite bakery café. It's the early-evening lull before late commuters come in for dinner, and the relaxed atmosphere here is like a warm towel on my mind. We buy a discounted bag of assorted day-old cookies from a quietly polite staff member. Then we linger in the homey interior of worn wooden chairs and tables arranged compactly about the white tile floor, this cozy atmosphere made even snug by the autumn chill outside. Sitting at the window-side counter for a while with our bag of cookies in front of us, she and I seem to be re-enacting a scene frequently found in our bygone days—all the times you and I would linger here, in the sweet aromas and chatter of convivial denizens long after we had finished our croissants and coffee.

"It's always comforting to be in this place," she says, arms crossed as she leans on the glass counter.

I turn to face her, draping my arm over the back of the chair I'm sitting in.

"True," I murmur. "It's such a soothing pocket of nostalgia. Like an idealistic memory embedded in the turbulence of the modern world."

"Yeah. And I wouldn't get to come here if it weren't for you. I'd be confined largely to the back of a particular mind, repressed."

I nod solemnly. You've given me every indication your disownment of her still stands.

Once we're home, she goes straight to the fridge and takes out a bottle of summer ale I'd forgotten all about. Your latest left-behind self emerges from the study, where he's undoubtedly been reading for much of the day.

He leans against the kitchen wall and asks, "How was work? Good meeting?"

I hand him the bag of cookies.

Who you were a couple years ago immediately answers, "Yeah, good."

Emphatically she twists the cap off the beer bottle, then she elaborates.

"The meeting was *excellent*, in fact. *If* you like your meetings to be sessions of post-hoc rationalization and future-projected complacency driven by unwarranted visionary's narcissism capable of only incremental progress."

"Well, I'm sorry that everyone else isn't as pragmatically tactical as you, and sorry that the world doesn't keep pace with your thoughts," he says.

She takes a gulp of beer, then rebuts with, "It's their job to move the field forward. They're not being paid to stagnate and make the organization's endeavors flashy but ill-performing vehicles for their obese egos."

"Don't argue," I tell them. They both have their points, but I don't want to get into those now.

"All right, all right," she says and holds the bottle out towards me.

I take it and gulp down what feels like a delicious mouthful of relaxing nostalgia. It prompts me to go see the oldest self of yours here. I hand the bottle back to your vocal former self. I turn to leave the kitchen, and who you've been recently opens the bag and takes out a brownie pillow cookie, still one of your favorites.

She's in the beanbag again, gazing out the bedroom window at a scene of oak trees and small hillside houses delectably rendered in orange tones by the setting sun. The view outside makes the creamy blue walls scantly adorned with posters and maps appear drab and all too flat.

"I'm tired of waiting," she says quietly.

As the oldest, she's spent the most time apart from you, some of her emotions amplified and others diminished by that time.

Standing beside her, I place a hand on her shoulder and answer, "I understand how you feel."

And I'm certain that I do. So many of us are impatient to be taken back by someone or something. For me, it's the world. I'm anxious to be again part of this vast something, the collection of someones that now holds me at arm's length ever since I spurned the communities and ecosystems around me that I had the luxury to take for granted, a wealth I spent frivolously.

I don't know if you'll ever take her back. Maybe by the time you do, I won't want you to have her.

She continues to stare at the bit of neighborhood visible through the window.

"You know," she says with a quiet, bright confidence. "There's something supremely gorgeous about the sheen of late-day sunlight on oak leaves."

"I know," I answer quietly but firmly, assuring her I understand, wanting to assure of something else that I cannot.

I don't understand how you don't miss her, how you can feel whole without her.

As the Past Tries to Catch Up
With You: Part 2

"Well, aren't you quite the customer," a voice I'd recognize anywhere says from across the table. "Patronizing almost daily, having such delightful rapport with the waitress," the voice continues as I lower my book, these words quashing all my interactions and activities here into a simplistic statement.

I look her in the eyes, and nostalgia envelops me like a gust of wind that's jarring but refreshing.

"If I didn't know better, I'd say you're interested in her. But she's not your type, is she?" your former self asks, anachronistic amid this scene of my present life.

"Seems then I'm not the only one who's been frequenting my favorite café recently," I reply, smiling unexpectedly.

"Well, we can talk about my presence here later. Right now, I need to know about his apparent absence. Where is he?"

"He didn't tell me."

"I always told you everything."

"Well, he decided to discontinue that habit—decided to have more discretion, to become more private."

"That seems unfortunate. We were so close."

"Yes, I do miss that," I agree wistfully.

"I'd like to think we're still close."

"We could be."

I sip from my mug of coffee. Her eyes peer into mine.

"I really want to trust you—I'm sure I can—but under the circumstances, I have to be as careful as possible. So sorry, I'm going to have to straight-out ask you. Are you telling me the truth?"

"Yes. He made sure that was really the only option I had. So I wouldn't be placed in a position to choose between you or him."

"Thanks. I'd like to think you'd choose me over him, but I don't know what's gone on between you two."

"It'd be a difficult choice. Let's leave it at that."

"Okay," she answers, nodding.

"So, where are you staying?" I ask, switching to a relevant but different subject.

"I'm renting out a small place in the Connectionist District."

"You're welcome to stay at my place if you want," I offer.

She leans forward to scrutinize me for a moment then says, "And this isn't some plan hatched by you and him to slow down my pursuit? A way to buy him more time to put more distance between us?"

"It would be no more a delay than your continued presence here is. If you were in such a hurry to catch up with him, you wouldn't still be here. Unless you've completely lost the trail. The fact that we're having this conversation now or at all means that you haven't been able to figure out anything. Clearly you've had time to learn my habits and routines here. There's no way you'd bother doing that if you weren't out of leads."

She concedes a grin.

"Astute as ever."

"Thanks," I say with a shrug.

After a moment, she says, "All right, I'll take you up on your offer. I don't have much money at the moment. Once he noticed that I had withdrawn a chunk of money from his bank account, he changed all his access codes."

"I figured the cost of tracking your future self would add up."

"Right. To cover my expenses and save up some money to continue traveling, I've taken on part-time work mapping out plausibility subspaces of possibility spaces."

"Well, at least you get to do something you're proficient in and enjoy."

"True, but financially it would be much easier if he had ex-friends in this area. Staying with an ex-friend would save me loads of money, and there'd be no awkwardness since he doesn't keep in contact with x.f.'s. But I don't know anyone here, except you. And I hadn't expected you to be here at all."

"Seems that meeting like this is rather strange for both of us then."

"I'd say so. When he left me behind, he also let entropy run its course with the vast majority of relationships we had. I assumed he let ties with you languish too, which would have been especially easy after you moved away. But as it turns out, you are the only one from that era he's still close with."

"An almost clean start has done him some good," I have to say.

"Good in his valuational system."

"We can only hope that our respective values coincide enough to be of mutual benefit."

"No, it's not enough to hope. You have to work towards common values or at least conventions."

"Yes, but ultimately our values and how we act upon them are matters of personal choice."

"Don't be so permissive. It doesn't suit you. Your disregard of social context is appalling. When did you become such an individualist?"

I have to give the question some thought, but then I'm able to pinpoint the shift.

"Since coming here," I answer, "Individualism has often been necessary in the absence of a robust sense of community."

"You shouldn't have left."

I sigh, almost smelling in the air here the wood and dirt of those summer days we shared.

"I mostly agree with you now," I admit. "But I couldn't have agreed with you back then. And it's been important to have been in the places that led me here."

"And is it still important to be here?"

"In one particular way it is. This is one of the few places where the work I'm doing can be done."

"Fair enough."

I sip more coffee as a wistful mood overcomes you.

"You should visit sometime," you murmur. "It's still so vibrant. You'd love it."

"That's what I'm afraid of. That I'd get overwhelmingly sentimental. Even talking with you now makes my heart ache."

Your eyes lose their intensity, reaching out to me with sympathy.

"I know. You've always been sensitive to reminders of what's come and gone. Prone to longing like no other," you reminisce, like you're talking about the mythic era of my childhood.

I nod, then you add, "Well, I'm glad we could meet again, even under these circumstances."

"I have to agree with you."

Autumn settles into the region while we settle into patterns of sharing our mornings and evenings in the cozy rooms of my apartment—our lives diverging daily when we depart for our respective jobs, coinciding again after business hours. Through the course of sharing time and space, I become acquainted with habits of yours I've never been exposed to. My once mundane moments turn into opportunities to observe your lifestyle. When entering the living room one evening, I find you clipping your toenails (which I do in the privacy of my bedroom).

Sometimes, as I prepare my morning bowl of granola, you're meticulously laying out or revising your budget for the week on the kitchen table. A couple times after work, I'll want to take a shower, and you're soaking in the tub to weave your thoughts and emotions together into a tight mental mesh of narrative memory. These episodes add to my knowledge of you, reshaping my long-inert conception of who you were into consideration of who you are.

Seldom do we talk about the pursuit. Mostly because you've been unable to turn up any new clues, and there is little I can contribute.

"His social style has been highly compartmentalized," I told you early on in our relationship as roommates, while we lounged on the sofa binging on asparagus chips as we do too often together.

"He likes to keep his various social situations separate, completely abandoning the alternately individual and integrated approach you prefer," I elaborated. "One result was that the depth of our interpersonal engagement was undiluted and uncomplicated by additional parties. But typically that depth was limited to only a few dimensions of our personalities, mostly introspective and philosophical ones. There weren't other people to bring additional dimensions like artistic creativity into play."

"I see," you murmured, considering this.

"Only briefly have I met a few of his friends in passing, but I know almost nothing about them. Occasionally, he'd mention a factoid about one of his friends or colleagues, and to be honest, I was almost entirely uninterested because he never told me enough about any of them for me to have enough context to understand the deeper significance of the tidbits he'd share."

"Do you think he had such a fragmented social life to make it difficult for me to find information about him?" you asked.

The inquiry struck me as unduly egocentric.

"That's possible, but I think he just found it more manageable to keep the people he knew socially separate," I replied. "And this separation was made all the easier by the urban landscape here. People here inhabit disparate neighborhoods that aren't well connected by the city's antiquated system of streets, and there are few spaces that bring them together. I hardly see anyone from work anywhere outside the office."

"That does make me wonder what kind of social habits I'd have here," you remarked. "If the structure of the city isn't conducive to getting people together, maybe I'd end up being really frustrated trying to do things with friends, as a group."

"I feel like this touches upon something that I've considered on and off," I mused aloud.

My eyes darted away from yours, as if to look for space for my thoughts to take shape in. I stared at the corner of the room to my right and continued.

"We're basically inhabiting societal structures after crucial phase transitions have occurred. One structure is what we've just been talking about, the solidification of a city's layout. But that seems to include another critical transformation. Before we had large cities and complex commercial systems, people lived in close proximity to each other in small communities. But as the population grew, it was possible to have increased specialization and decreased overt interdependence."

My eyes returned to you, now needing yours. Seeing the tacit agreement in your relaxed and attentive posture, I went on.

"And at some point, it was impossible to know everyone in the community, and our reliance upon each other is now mediated by financial transactions or other codified interactions that make it unnecessary to know people at an individual, personal level. Because we're living in a time after these fundamental changes reshaped human activities on basic levels, some choices—like how we socialize—have been to some degree made for us. To a larger degree in some places than others."

"In other words, here it's easier to embrace the anonymity and isolation offered to us by the shift society has long since undertaken to an economic system of specialization," you concluded.

"Yes, contemporary society's structure has been set up for that. You have to put in significant effort to overcome the momentum social expectations impart on you."

"You talk about this like it's all just a collection of rules that broadly apply or are followed without objection. But isn't this a case of scale confusion? Individuals infer how to interact based on the much larger system they perceive themselves to be a part of, when instead, they could be considering how to interact more as individuals."

"Who's the individualist now?" I quipped with a grin. You gave me an emphatic shove on the shoulder.

"But seriously, the behaviors of both individuals and the systems they create emerge from each other," I then said. "But a large system with established, pervasive patterns has tremendous influence over those behaviors."

"Of course. I just meant that there are inextricably individual aspects to our interactions."

I brought my right foot up upon the edge of the sofa cushion and wrapped my hands around the knee.

"Yes, those aspects still exist," I then said. "But they are circumscribed by us, often unconsciously, because we're entwined with structures of the societal scale."

"Maybe we need to remind or prod each other to stop that circumscription, at least once in a while," you suggested.

I nodded thoughtfully.

We left it at that, and you went to soak in the tub.

That was the first of many discussions on the subject of interpersonal relations. We frequently talk about the nature of social interactions as you become better acquainted with the facets of this city, but these discussions rarely involve your future self.

Weight and Warmth

During our break between shifts at the dream cannery today, we sit on our usual rooftop bench and stare up at the clouds. The autumn sunlight gives everything here, including us, that subtle golden sheen I wish could last forever but foreshadows winter.

"I really should've thrown out this underwear so there'd be no danger of ever putting it on again," you grouse, your words emphatic but sluggish, lacking their usual fluidity.

"It's old?" I ask, murmuring the question skyward.

"The thing is a holdover from bygone days," you tell me. "It's basically a wardrobe anachronism I keep around in case I desperately need an extra. But now it's become an enabler of laundry laziness. Instead of doing the wash, I used up all my underwear and put this one on thinking it wouldn't be too bad. But it's not giving my heart nearly enough support. I feel all droopy and floppy."

I blush at these intimate details, and instantly the almost-chilly air doesn't feel cool at all.

"Sounds uncomfortable," is all I can say.

"Seriously, it feels like I've got a ton of secrets that I need to get off my chest. Secrets made of bricks. I'm getting rid of this thing tonight—the moment I'm done with my laundry."

Despite the fatigue in your voice, your words rapidly impart upon me the heat of your thoughts. It's like a gust of hot air from the cannery's crucible, and it evokes my memories of the first time I felt this warmth from you, how stunned I was by the suddenness of the temperature change.

That was years ago, in third grade, just after our class had read the story of "the greedy inventor" together. Our teacher Ms. Crofäteno was nudging us into a discussion with questions she had written on the chalkboard. One of them—I forget what exactly—crystallized my thoughts and compelled me to share this gem now in my possession. I felt cleverly sure that the inventor was a well-intentioned but deeply misguided control freak, and so I revealed this sparkling idea for our class to consider—admire.

Ms. Crofäteno nodded thoughtfully at my offering, waiting—hoping for a response our classmates were reluctant to offer. But in those quiet, listless moments that lay between us and the end of the school day, my interpretation remained alone. Until, to my surprise, your thoughts leapt on to the scene—a startling, complementary counterpoint that declared the inventor a misunderstood genius. Though their contact was tenuous, curtailed by the ringing of the school bell, our thoughts exchanged between us that crucial glow of our minds.

That was the beginning of those years when you would daydream for both of us. When you expanded my world from the small bubble of residential blocks centered around the little green house on Gliss Avenue that I still call home. When you turned my days into a series of adventures you'd launch us into every chance you'd get.

Looking at you now, I know you could do that again. Though not right this very moment. If captured on canvas or in a photo, your face could become a timeless portrait of quiet annoyance.

I'm about to sheepishly suggest that we could switch underwear. I don't need as much support since my heart isn't as heavy as yours.

But before I can figure out how to mention any of this, you say to me, "Let me lean on you for just a little while, then I'll feel better."

"Okay," I reply.

Then I feel the weight of your being press on me. A moment later, the warmth of your thoughts has worked its way through my psyche to touch mine, yet again.

Spilt Secrets

I remember how we lingered in the tree-shaded alley behind the building that houses the Department of Cognitive Archaeology that afternoon. Like we had no plans for the rest of the day and could just dwell in intrigue.

You were the one who spotted it from down the path, and moments later, there it lay between us on the narrow concrete walkway of this quieter, sparser, less-frequented part of campus. A dark puddle of spilt secrets. We stared at this once-concealed knowledge just inches from our feet. A few clusters of maple tree flowers floated like miniature bouquets on this murk which gleamed slightly with late-day sunlight.

"Do you think this belongs to anyone we know?" you asked.

"Probably not. Everyone we know is really careful with their secrets," I answered.

"True, but maybe there was some kind of accident."

"Maybe."

We continued to stare at the inky little pool, mesmerized by its unknown depths. My mind conjured up a scenario for this puddle's origins: a fellow student fatigued by consecutive all-nighters pulled for class projects, sluggishly and unsteadily he treads his path, in danger of being crumpled to the ground by the hefty, swaying under the unbalanced psychological load he bears, secrets sloshing out of his psyche.

Before I could finish this imaginary scene, my attention was jerked back to reality by your foot reaching out toward the secrets.

"Hey! Be careful!" I shouted. "It could be really deep."

"It's okay," you assured me. "I'm just going to prod it a bit."

The tip of your shoe touched the surface of the secrets, and you tried to stir the goo a bit.

"It's pretty thick," you told me as I watched your shoe produce sluggish ripples.

Becoming a bit bolder, you put a little more of your shoe into it, until about half the sole was submerged.

After getting a feel for how dense the secrets were, you tried to pull your foot away, but the stuff was much stickier than you expected, holding fast to the bottom of your shoe as you managed to lift your foot only slightly. Thick, dark strands tethered your shoe to the puddle. As you continued to slowly raise your foot, these filaments elongated, like gelatinous, obsidian tentacles reaching out of the depths. Suddenly, these secrets clinging your shoe contracted and yanked your foot downward, disrupting your balance. You stumbled forward, right into the puddle, up to your knees in it.

"Oh dang," I muttered.

"Okay, yeah, this definitely doesn't belong to anyone we know," was all you said.

Your words made it clear that the secrets had already permeated into your psyche.

I reached out a hand, which you grasped as you leaned towards me. I braced myself and pulled firmly. Slowly, you lifted your left leg. With our hands locked and arms tense, I felt you strain against the secrets. They were obstinately viscous, as if trying to claim you as their new bearer. You got your left foot out of the muck and planted it just beyond the periphery of the secrets, right in front of me. Gradually, your right leg rose out of that thick darkness, pulling with it a thick layer of goop that clung to the bottom half of your right pant leg. Finally, your right foot emerged and joined your left one on the patch of sidewalk just before me. We let go of each other, and I assessed the situation. The bottom third of your pants were heavily covered by a coat of secrets.

"So, back to the dorm then," I concluded. There was no way you were going anywhere else in this state.

"Yeah," you replied.

We started walking towards the building we had called home for the past year, at what felt like the most lethargic pace ever. Your steps were sluggish, slowed by the weight of the secrets plastering your pants and shoes.

"So, what was that all about?" I asked.

"You don't want to know," you said, almost whispering. "Let me just say I think I know why those secrets are there. I certainly wouldn't want to keep them."

Then, noticing you wince, I asked, "Are you going to be all right?"

"I think so. I'll feel better after I wash this off."

"But what about the stuff that's already gotten under your skin?"

I wondered if we should be heading towards health services instead.

"If I haven't had an inflammatory response by now, it can't get much worse," you said. "I'll just have to let my psyche break down this nastiness. It'll be probably subtly disquieting, in the form of unsettling dreams for a few nights. But nothing more."

I still had doubts. While your emotional constitution had always proven itself to be robust, secrets can be insidious, taking their time to stealthily plague swaths of the psyche.

Then, though I couldn't be entirely sure, you appeared to be shivering slightly, a bodily motion that struck me as anachronistic in warmth of late spring.

Good thing it's not yet hot enough to wear shorts, I thought for just a moment, then considered offering you my pants to mitigate some of your discomfort—we could change behind some shrubbery beside the path. I immediately realized that this was a barely—if at all—appropriate course of action. While I wouldn't have minded walking the rest of the way with my flannel shirt wrapped around my pants-less legs, that might lead to more trouble; the rumor mill would undoubtedly churn out nuggets of gossip for weeks. Perhaps even proposing this swap would forever alter our relationship. So I said nothing of this thought.

Keeping pace with your stifled but still resolute steps, I simply waited for you to say something else, which you didn't. Leaving me to think—as we drew gradually, almost lazily closer to the dormitory—that I should keep a close eye on you for a while, forming a secret of my own. A promise I still keep.

Alloparenting Brainchildren

"Hey, want to go bolster the economy with some materialistic consumption after work?" I ask.

Because I probably won't get another chance today. Our lunch break is drawing to a close with the leisurely sipping of coffee in the nearly vacant cafeteria.

"I'd love a little mindless transacting, but I can't. I have to take care of The Ideas tonight," you reply, thrusting me back into the reality that I become utterly detached from when we're pursuing lucrative enterprises for our corporate conglomerate. To make ends meet, you've had to adopt some ideas, to supplement your salary so that the executive board members' salaries can continue to be competitive.

"Oh," I murmur.

"Yeah, have to help them develop and all that."

I nod as you drink some coffee, then I finally ask the question provoked in my mind every time you bring up these ideas.

"Do you ever feel, well... weird nurturing other people's ideas?"

"To be honest," you begin. "Yeah, sometimes. I definitely care about these ideas, but I'm sure it's not the same as having my own ideas. But it's also preparing me for when I have my own ideas, someday."

"I see... I've just been curious how you feel about them. You know, you give them so much time and attention, you must have a deep bond with them, but they didn't emerge from your mind," I say, wondering if I sound naïve or ignorant to you. "And later, you might not even see them much, once they've matured and go their own ways, off into the world."

"Yeah, occasionally I do have difficulties with this relationship. There are times when I can't help but feel so strongly about The Ideas—you know, really attached to and protective of them. Those feelings can well up so quickly and unexpectedly. It might take only a moment, like when I see these ideas trying to explain things, form patterns and reach conclusions.

"Or when I think about how much they've grown and how important they might become. And all too rapidly, I'm absolutely convinced that I'd care about these ideas no matter what— regardless of my personal circumstances or whether I'm being paid to foster them. I can't help but adore this one brilliant artistic idea that aspires to one day be a principle and join together with other ideas to form a theory."

You're beaming as you mention this one you're very fond of, but all too soon, your expression changes.

"Then, there's the other end of the spectrum, when The Ideas just totally *annoy* me, and I don't want to deal with them at all. When they're restless, uncooperative or don't get along with each other. Sometimes, they just want things their way."

"Doesn't that make you worry about how you'll deal with your own ideas in the future?"

"Yeah, it does, but like I said, this is a kind of training for that. I've learned—the hard way—to be more critical, self-possessed and frank when these ideas get too audacious or crazy."

"So there are times when you've had to get some of these ideas to shape up… like, forcefully?"

"Definitely. A few have been totally overindulged, used to being entertained all the time. Sometimes you have to be harsh. And ultimately, it's for their own good. I don't want them becoming all pompous and condescendingly grandiose."

I nod, thinking this over. Knowing I have a weakness for aspiring, fledgling ideas, a propensity to coddle the precocious ideas of friends and family with fascination and consideration, I wonder if I'd be any good at fostering ideas placed in my care.

"You'll be a good thinker," I tell you, then hastily add, "I mean, I'm sure you already are. You'll only get better and have wonderful ideas of your own in the future."

"Oh, well, thanks," you say, smiling and nodding.

"Actually," you quietly add after a moment. "I've decided to start having ideas of my own as soon as possible. I really don't want to wait any longer, especially now that I have a better sense of just how much time and effort ideas need."

I stare at you nonplussed, startled that the someday you only vaguely mentioned now seems a lot sooner than I expected.

"I haven't decided on any definite plans yet, but I'm trying to figure things out now. Don't tell anyone. I probably won't break the news to people here until after the ideas are conceived—you know, when they're gestating."

"Okay," I murmur.

Staring at the rows of unoccupied tables and chairs before us, dazed by the revelation of your intentions, I imagine you devoting everything to your growing ideas, wondering if you will be hesitant to entrust them to others even briefly, or if you will eagerly invite many of us to be part of the joys and challenges young ideas will bring into your life.

I'm curious if I will play any role in the development of your ideas. I'd like to be a part of their maturation, even if only peripherally. I hope you'll let me. I can't wait to get to know them.

Under the Influence

While I'm on my way to take the SEDE (Socioeconomic Echelon Determination Exam), we spot each other amid the bustle of city dwellers, and you wave to me.

I grow nervous as we approach one another. I wonder if I should concoct some excuse to brush you off. I don't want to be rude to you, but I'm fearful of the consequences our encounter could have.

Then, before I know it, we're somehow standing face to face in the corner of the hydroponics plaza.

"Exam day, right?" you ask. "You're heading to the testing center?"

"You got it," I reply, nodding, trying not to make too much eye contact.

"Okay, well, I don't want to keep you then," you reply, easing my worry—my dread.

"Cool. Maybe we can go hiking this weekend or bake some scones," I suggest.

"Sounds good," you agree. "Good luck!"

The moment you say those well-wishing words, I hastily avert my gaze. But it's too late. I've fleetingly caught a glimpse of your exuberant smile—radiant in the morning sunlight—and the beautiful sight launches me into a heady euphoria.

"Thanks," I manage to murmur, my mind aswirl.

"See you later!"

You head off, probably to the workshop, and I walk tipsily towards the testing location. Palms tingling, heart uttering deliriously, I hope I can sober up before the arduous test begins.

But sadly, I become only further inebriated by the time I sit down at a small desk of laminated particleboard, taking my place amid rows of fellow test-takers. I stare giddily at the test booklet before me, elated by your smile and afraid of what lurks upon the pages in this slim volume of evaluative text. In my current state of mind, the questions I'll soon be faced with are likely to condemn me to some lower rung of our society.

"You may begin," announces the test proctor from the front of the room.

I take a deep breath and open the booklet. I might as well do what I can. There's still a chance I'll regain my sensibility during the test, or enough of it to land upon some hierarchical level close to my peers.

Then, as I read the test questions on the first page, I'm stunned by their facile nature. They're just utterly pedestrian. The most complicated-looking question borders on the absurd:

A 32-year-old man loans his 7-year-old nephew 250 moiters at a monthly interest rate of 1.5%. If the nephew pays back with interest only 42 moiters after the first month and then 73 moiters 3 months later, two years after the loan was made, what would the man's nephew's age be?

(a) 34   (b) 193   (c) 357   (d) 9

Maybe it's just the beginning that's like this, to ease us into the gnarled, confounding heart of the test. But as I flip through the booklet, the entire test seems to be bafflingly simple.

Bowled over, I immediately raise my hand.

"Something the matter?" the proctor whispers, coming up beside me.

"I think I have a misprinted test booklet. Or a booklet for another kind of test," I tell her.

I hold the open booklet out towards the proctor. She inspects the contents, then examines the barcode on the back cover.

"Everything looks in order here," she tells me.

"Oh," I murmur.

She gives me a concerned look and says, "I hope you didn't study the wrong materials or sign up for the wrong test."

"No… I must, you know, just be… nervous," I reply.

"All right. Just calm down, and hopefully it'll look less intimidating," she advises, handing me back the booklet.

"Okay, thanks."

So I just get to work answering the oddly juvenile questions.

Halfway through the exam, I start to wonder if this is some psychological experiment or bizarre joke.

And then it dawns on me.

Your smile may have altered my cognition so that the test questions are conformally mapping to simpler isomorphs on an unconscious level. This would make my conscious test-taking experience stunningly easy. If so, hopefully the mapping preserves the inferential structures and thereby the correctness of the answers I'm now selecting.

Two thirds of the way through the exam, the questions become noticeably more difficult, more like the practice questions I've been working on for months. The effects of your smile are probably wearing off, and I wonder if I should have indulged myself more fully in it. Would that have made the exam even more of a breeze? Then again, becoming too exhilarated by your smile would no doubt have left me nearly incapacitated, as has happened in the past.

When I've got about three quarters of the exam done, the questions are as challenging as they can get. Fortunately, I've still got a sizable swath of time left to work through them carefully.

I finish with time to spare. So I go back to the beginning of the exam and look over the questions there, finding them far more complex than the ones I answered at the start. Anxiously, I work through a couple, and much to my relief, I get answers that end up corresponding to the same multiple-choice letters I selected earlier! I check over as many test questions as I can in the remaining time and uncover only a couple discrepancies.

"Close your test booklets," the proctor announces when I've checked a little more than a third of my test answers.

I fold the booklet shut and take a deep breath.

Now I'll simply have to wait for the test results and see which stratum of our society your smile places me upon.

As the Past Tries to Catch Up
With You: Part 3

The day he left, you went into his apartment. His hasty departure that allowed you to easily enter; from outside, he couldn't lock the window he had used to access the fire escape, guaranteeing you success when you tried the fire-escape-entry maneuver you first used that time you went out to the laundromat and forgot to bring your keys.

Once inside, you stayed there, expecting him to be back in the evening. As you awaited his return, you went through his diligently kept financial records, a stack of recent mail, chronologically shelved notebooks. Whatever was accessible to you.

When you took stock of the densely scribbled notes on his wall calendar, you were impressed by the busy schedule he kept. Then you spotted my name written on several dates along with the names of cafés or parks where we had planned to meet. That's when you knew I was here. Your eyes widened, and you relished the smile warming your face.

Inspecting the artifacts of his recent life, you gained a sense of the identity he had forged here. The choice of appliances, arrangement of furniture and assortment of foods in the kitchen all gave you glimpses of his lifestyle and personal predilections.

But of course, what most appealed to your curiosity were the items more deeply entwined with mental activities. What began as casually browsing the narratives he had amassed in the course of satiating his intellectual appetite became sheer absorption as you found practically every item in his literature collection fascinating, evidence that you still share the same tastes in culture. Then, as if the most substantial matter had been saved for last, you examined the work-related articles he had set out on his worktable nestled in the corner of the cozy studio space he had at the back of his apartment. Rapidly you were engrossed by the schematics he was drafting for his latest client, a rough plan for a fantastical mental refuge from the ordinary—likely for someone deeply embedded in the matrix of mainstream society. You pored over anything you could find— sketches, notes and reports—to understand the occupation he had taken up.

As the hours went by, fatigue set in, and you succumbed to sleep while reclining in the lounge chair you bought with your first paycheck for plausibility mapping (which you had been delighted to see that he kept). The next morning, you went out to your part-time job, deciding to pay another visit soon, thinking he might be on a short trip or spending the night at the residence of a romantic partner.

You went back a couple days later, once again climbing up the fire escape. When you reached it, you found the window left open to air out an empty living room. You stood on the fire escape for several minutes, staring into the vacated space, dumbfounded. Then you went in and looked around, full of utter disbelief as you walked through his completely cleaned out apartment. You figured he must have stealthily returned and expediently removed everything or had someone he knows take care of that.

When you told me all this, I was impressed. I thought he'd be mailing in checks for rent until he could slip back into the city or coordinate some other way to deal with his apartment.

Months later, we still don't have a good idea of how he cleared his belongings out so quickly, of what happened to all those things that had inhabited what is now no longer his space.

I don't have a fire escape. Instead, there is a small veranda outside my living room.

This afternoon, I walk into the living room to find you standing on it, looking out at the city made resplendent by the setting sun. The air is that tantalizing shade of chilliness—cold enough to be brisk but warm enough to engender an ambiance of leisure and even wonder, a temperature of almost timeless quality, as if enveloped in this air we could hover indefinitely at the brink of autumn's most hospitable twilight.

Leaning on the parapet, eyes locked in enchanted city-gazing, you seem to be in a state of mind that combines relaxed observation and thoughtful reflection. Perhaps you're wondering about what awaits out there in places you haven't explored yet, or about the possibility that he's somewhere amid those buildings and streets, hidden in the convolutions of the urban environment, nestled in the nook of an obscure, fringe social circle.

Enticed by what strikes me as a tacit conversation among you, autumn and the cityscape, I decide to join in—or at least eavesdrop more extensively on—this amiable dialogue. Maybe it's a private conversation that I'll be an unwanted hinderance to, but it compels me so convincingly to draw closer, to be unsatisfied with anything short of being out there beside you.

I slide the veranda's glass door open and step out, then close the door behind me.

"Hey," you murmur, eyes still on the metropolis.

"Hey," I echo.

Standing beside you, I lean forward, pressing my folded arms upon the parapet, considering again the season which enfolds everything here.

While autumn's cool days, late-blooming asters and brilliant foliage pleasantly complements your presence, spring is the season that would best suit you here. That time of gentle warmth and renewed vitality when the streets become replete with people, color and possibilities, the city filling out again. But that is still many months away, and if he's not here then, you won't be either—if you can help it. Which is unfortunate.

At least you came here when the city's vibrance was in full swing, but now we are all heading once again towards the more quiescent state we are—or at least I am never quite ready for.

You remain quiet as though in telepathic communion with the city.

I think about the glimpses I've caught of your private language, instances of thoughts linguistically rendered for your own use: your journal left open on the kitchen table; notes scribbled on receipts lying atop the heap of magazines to be recycled; sheets torn from sketchpads, sprawled out upon sofa cushions. These artifacts always pique my interest in the representational system you employ to give your cognition form on paper. All too easily, I become mesmerized by those amalgams of curvy and angular symbols that encode your ideas.

I wonder what it would be like to converse with you in this language, to exchange our thoughts in expressions you are fluent in. Doing so would confer upon our relationship a degree of intimacy that you have only with your selves. How much of that intimacy, I wonder, is still possible with your future self? Perhaps he has adopted a new dialect.

Overly Openhearted

A

From within your open medicine cabinet, at eye-level, it unswervingly confronts me, demanding and holding my attention, as if we're locked in a stare off. Like it knows what it's doing to me and hasn't any qualms about that. And what it's doing is changing my perspective, as if its widening of my eyes permits me to see what I haven't.

It all makes *almost* complete sense now: why you've seemed so very *you* in the past week, more emotionally generous and receptive. Why there's even more resonance with you. Why you're prone to oversharing like never before: verbally, emotionally and temporally offering more than you should of your life—which I alternately adore and deplore; I'm delighted when I can bask in your ebullience but appalled when your frustrations are spewed upon me. I thought it was just your mood, a phase of empathic (over-)abundance, perhaps influenced by an intensified exercise routine.

But now this bottle of cardiac dilator before me foists itself upon me as the unthwartable explanation of your then-subtle, now-obvious transformation.

It supplies, however, no explanation of itself. There's never been any apparent reason for you to take CarDi. As long as I've known you, your heart has always been sufficiently, even generously open. You always take in emotions from the swath of world wrapped around you, taking them seriously, and outpourings of your feelings are not uncommon. But maybe that's all been thanks to CarDi, and now you've upped the dosage or switched to a stronger brand...

"Did you find the contact solution?" you ask. "It's been like ten minutes."

"Um, yeah, I got it," I hastily answer, eyes still focused on the medication.

But your words have dislodged me sufficiently from the field of fixation emanating from this container of pills, enough to reorient my thoughts to the task at hand—getting the contact solution I need to smooth over the emotionally frayed cardiac regions, to preempt irritation and grating, to continue our heart-to-heart without aggravation. Breaking my visual engagement with the meds, I grab the jar of contact solution off the shelf of psyche care products. I apply it generously to the raw areas of my psyche, then head back to the living room, with the jar in hand, just in case. It could be a while, especially with you dilated.

B

As I head home, I feel like the cardiac dilator in your medicine cabinet is commanding my attention from down the street—a formidable distance for a small, inanimate object. It displaces thoughts of tomorrow's plans with concerns about why you are using these metaphysiology-modifying drugs. And because taking my customary route home down the river requires little cognitive effort, my mind is amply able to consider the CarDi sitting in your bathroom. And the lulling light of evening encourages me to leisurely do so.

So I scan memories for clues, for any evidence of the usual circumstances cardiac dilators are beneficial for:

1. rocky relationships needing improved bidirectional transfer of emotions and
2. constriction of the heart limiting the intake of emotions, usually positive ones.

Retrospectively reviewing the social interactions of yours that I've observed and that you've mentioned, I mentally draft a report on your interpersonal state of affairs, summarizing your psychological status for each entity in your socioscape—parents, community groups, creative teams, close friends. But this distillation, while an interesting updating of mental models, yields no insight. It's really just the status quo, plus the effects I'd expect from CarDi: increased emotional dispersion and absorption. So far as I can discern, even from a highly speculative or paranoid vantage point, there's nothing even vaguely suggestive of 1 or 2. Except working with the new fractal geometrist on your project team, which is expectedly awkward, and that's hardly enough to warrant taking CarDi.

The results are frustrating yet reassuring—perhaps frustratingly reassuring and reassuringly frustrating. I want all the more desperately to know what's going on, but there's nothing obviously wrong, so it can't be that bad, unless you are expertly concealing something.

I opt to feel frustratingly reassured, trusting that if there were some issue, you'd tell me.

C

I see the dilator's effects all the time now, like I've become attuned to a new color you've taken to painting with everywhere on the canvas of your social interactions. From store clerks to work colleagues to quirky acquaintances, you are ever affable and effusive. Yesterday in the gymnasium, you talked at length with some tween about the role of aerobic activity in parent-child relationships. I watched now and then from the high beam, then from the rings and finally from the bars.

I'm comfortable with but still curious about these circumstances.

Especially because the effects are never in the service of the two reasons cardiac dilator is typically used for. I have yet to glimpse any hint that there's a relationship greatly benefitting from increased emotional exchange or that you need increased absorption of positive emotions. In my observations, it's always largely the exuding or outrush of those warm emotions from you.

And then suddenly, while I'm eating a scallop and avocado dinner, I realize that's it: the pattern of persistent ebullience, it's the hallmark of being in love. But recognition of your probable psychological state is then all the more befuddling. Why would you be on a cardiac dilator if you're in love? Are you trying to diffuse away the emotions you would otherwise direct at your romantic interest? Spread those feelings of fondness across a swath of people to dissipate the intensity, to preempt deeper affections? Or are you trying to harness the glow of being in love to generally brighten your social interactions? What other explanations could there be?

There is one certainty that emerges from this nebulosity of inquiry. The situation must be shaped by who you are in love with. If I can figure out who has rendered this effect upon you, answers will emerge.

D

At the beach, there is no one but me to intercept the emotions radiating from your open heart while you reclined upon the shore's fine ivory grit, mind seemingly adrift among the clouds your eyes gaze up at. Delightfully, my skin is warmed by the sun as my heart is warmed by yours. What I don't absorb from your heart wanders its way out into the world, to drift in the air, undulate in ocean currents, seep into the sand. It's not unlike what's happening with my own heart as my work-related anxiety, nature-induced tranquility, pleasure of your company and nondescript wonderment escape away. Like we're two stars, you shining more intensely, emitting our energy into the surrounding, more rarefied matrix.

Who are you besotted with? I want to ask. Who could do this to you? The words stay within me, but my heart effuses this curiosity into my demeanor, slightly charging the air around me before wafting away with the sea breeze.

Being here, it's difficult to think that there's the entire rest of the world that our backs are now turned to. I feel like this could be it. Just an expanse of sky and ocean, then a narrow margin of sand, a strip of green behind that, the birds and you and me.

"Funny how there is no organism we know of that's cloud-like, nothing existing as a kind of consciously motile nebula, yet we can imagine what that might be like," you muse.

"Yes, I suppose jellyfishes are the closest to your description, and even they don't really resemble clouds," I answer.

"Exactly."

You close your eyes, perhaps to imagine wispy, mist-like creatures.

"How about some fries later?" you murmur.

"Yeah, I could go for some," I answer, knowing what you really crave is ketchup and something to go with it, to mitigate the sweet, savory tartness and thick liquidy texture.

E

As we leisurely and intermittently pluck from a platter of delectable fries in the seaside cafe, our conversation meanders about, wending its way abstractly into the topic of regret.

"You know, I've been wondering every now and then how much I should regret decisions I made in the distant past, when I was really young," I tell you. "Because I'm a different, hopefully better person now, and if I take that perspective seriously, I should feel less regret. Because we don't really regret the decisions of someone else, at least not as much as we regret our own decisions, right? Regret entails a sense of responsibility. We don't usually regret how things turned out if there was nothing we could have done about it. Regret is essentially feeling badly about a choice you made and assumes you could have chosen differently. So then what about choices made by who you were? How responsible are we for the choices of who we used to be if we've changed dramatically over time?"

Your eyes gleam with delight and affection, and you tell me, "Yes, I might know where you're heading with this. Let's see if I can shortcut a portion of the journey for you. I've been using the Regret Management practices I've learned from Aetera, and they've really helped me to have better relationships with my past selves and maybe even with my future selves. But I don't have any truly massive regrets, so I wonder how effective it will be for the outcomes of higher-stakes decisions."

I nod, starting to, I think, get the general idea. But one part of what you said has unrivaled salience, especially because you are now beaming in this recently familiar, characteristic way.

"Who's Aetera?" I ask.

"Oh, you've never read *The Interweaving of Causational Fields*?"

"I've been meaning to for a long time, but it's so dauntingly *epic*."

"Epic is part of what makes it good. What makes it *really* good is Aetera. She and her culture substantively and systematically engage dimensions of self—cognition, emotion, creativity…"

Then, as you describe away, I know what's going on. You talk about Aetera as if she is a peer you admire and take pride in, attuned vicariously with, as if she is a real person. And to you she is and more than that: a focal point for all your faith in humanity.

And she's it, the piece around which everything interlocks to make sense. Aetera must be why you need the cardiac dilator. The love you have for her can only be unrequited, and CarDi is one way to alleviate your heart of the powerful pressures the copious love exerts. Or perhaps this love is only requitable if poured out into humanity, for the positivity to be potentially reciprocated by us, the recipients and representatives to you of humanity.

"…like Generosity Coaching, Ambiguity Mapping and Regret Management, give her processes to avoid problematical emotional reflexes and to cultivate perspectives on her selves and their emotions—and better yet, develop more meaningful relationships with them," you continue, enthusiasm only rising. "Ones that complement the intuitive, natural workings of spontaneously occurring thoughts and feelings. Regret Management can improve or at least encourage reconsideration of our relationship with regret."

"This sounds like something I could use. That everyone could use," I remark, the last part of what you've said particularly piquing my attention.

"Oh, it certainly is."

"Tell me more."

"Well, it basically has two parts: pre-regret, and post-regret," you begin to explain. "What one can do in anticipation of regret and what one can do once regret has set in, after some decision has resulted in regret. Within pre-regret, there's preempting, contrasting and minimization…"

You explain away, gleefully, drawing me into Aetera's world.

Vacation from Visibility

You are disappearing. Rapidly. At this point, the parts of you not covered by clothing look like a reflection on a glass window, the sky behind you more salient than your face.

If you were an image on a computer screen, your opacity would be at 20%.

I try to talk you out of it, but you're set on vanishing, insisting that you need the invisibility.

"I'm tired of being a constant participant in the world. I need a break. To just observe things for a while," you tell me.

I almost expect your words to be as faint as you, but your voice is just the same as ever.

"But how are you going to do stuff like get groceries?" I ask, hoping to find a pragmatic reason for you to stay visible.

"I've stocked up on nonperishables, and my CSA shipments just get dropped off outside my door."

It occurs to me that you are being very transparent about your transparency, and though part of my mind is humored by this, I dismiss this like a teacher would ignore a remark made by the class clown to get on with the lesson at hand.

"Don't do it," I blurt. "People will forget about you. You'll lose the places you have in our lives and in the community. You'll have a hard time… re-integrating when you become visible again."

You smile, and the warmth in this expression makes me feel like I'm a precocious child who almost understands something I cannot yet fully appreciate. I wait for you to correct me by telling me your more memorable and important than I give you credit for.

Instead, you say, "That is very possible. But without relinquishing our habitation of certain spaces, it can be difficult for us to explore and settle into different spaces in each other's lives. And difficult for others to inhabit the lives of people we care about. That's why I'm not asking anyone here to save a place for me while I'm invisible. I know some will, but it feels unfair to ask. Our lives can only hold so much, and I don't want to have someone hold open a corner for me that would be better off filled."

I can't dispute what you've said, but it doesn't change how I see you: tenuous, a wisp of the person I've gotten to know so well. You look like you are only connected to the real world by the clothes you wear, given substance by the canvas jacket, beige t-shirt and jeans.

"But who knows," you say. "Maybe all I'll need is a week of invisibility, and I'll be rested enough to be a part of the world like I usually am."

"Or it could be months, and you'll wind up becoming alienated."

"Either way, I believe this needs to happen."

I nod out my acceptance.

Then I ask, "So what do you plan to observe during your stint of invisibility?"

"You know how I like to people watch."

I try for a moment to figure out if you're making some sort of joke.

"Don't worry," you assure me. "I'm not going to be stalking anyone. Nothing like that. I'll just be wandering the city, lounging on park benches, looking at who's around. I'll probably go on a lot of walks through the parks and around city neighborhoods, getting to know elements of the landscape and admiring the architecture of people's homes. I'm going to enjoy plenty of music too. There are all those concerts on the waterfront throughout the summer."

"That does sound nice."

"Doesn't it? So just think of me as being indefinitely on vacation or sabbatical."

The way you've tried to reframe the situation does ease my concerns but also prompts me to ask, "You didn't want to take an actual vacation?"

"I'd rather stay in a familiar environment and not go through all the trouble of packing and making travel arrangements."

I nod. I haven't been in the mood to travel lately either.

"Well, enjoy your vacation then," I find myself saying.

"Thanks. I'll let you know how it was once I'm back."

As the Past Tries to Catch Up
With You: Part 4

I wake up out of a dream where I was faced with a difficult choice. But the details of the decision don't make it into my first minute of consciousness. I'm left with only the the feeling of being caught between two compelling options. I lie in bed for a while, expecting sleep to envelop me at any moment, but it doesn't.

Eventually hunger sets in, and I head to the kitchen. In the dim yellow glow of the lamp on the corner table, I see you on the sofa with your journal in your lap. I'm surprised since you typically sleep soundly through the night.

"Hey," I murmur, voice kept down as if to match the lighting.

"Hey. I just suddenly woke up with all these thoughts in my mind," you tell me.

"I think my mind is full of pre-thoughts that will become thoughts any moment now," I reply. "Want to talk about yours?"

"Yeah, okay."

I sit down in the armchair beside the sofa.

"Mostly I've been thinking about what this might be like from his perspective," you begin. "Which basically means I've been thinking about what it'd be like for me if I were him, if I had some past self intent on nagging me. Which reminded me once again that my own thoughts do a good job of nagging me. If they didn't, I'm sure past selves of mine would be on my case like I'm on his.

"And I realized that basically the thoughts that nag me, well, I'm going after him so they can nag him through me. These thoughts that were once his when he was me, I'm trying to bring them back to him. I suppose it's like someone constantly trying to return something to you that you don't want or that you've outgrown. To put it simplistically, it's like I'm trying to give him back an old pair of shoes because I think they're really comfortable and look great on him, but he doesn't want them because he doesn't like the style or they don't fit well anymore."

"That is an interesting way of summing up aspects of this situation," I muse. "Or maybe another way to put it is that you're trying to get him to go back to somewhere that he's been, a place he doesn't want to be anymore."

"Yes, you could say that. Like I'm trying to get him to go back there so he can head from there in the direction that matters most."

"While he's moving in the direction that matters most to him."

"Right."

The tone of our conversation feels so serious, latent with consequence—as if developing the right analogy would reveal his whereabouts.

"Is there any chance you could find a direction that works for both of you?" I ask.

"Maybe, but he won't let me get close enough to even find out what direction he's headed in."

"It's too bad you didn't find me first. I might have been able to help. Like relay a message to him or drop some hints. Then he might not have freaked out and fled."

"Yeah, possibly. But you know how I like to be direct when I feel strongly about something."

"I've gotten to know that aspect of you a little too well."

You nod, the motion seems to me tinged with nostalgia. Perhaps you are thinking back to one of the frenzied arguments

I've been spectator to.

"How about some soumen?" I ask. "I'm feeling hungry."

"Sure, that'd be nice."

For a moment, I wonder if I am curtailing a discussion that could yield significant insight, but I quickly decide that if sleep can't be had, a light meal may do us some good. An empty stomach can easily lead the mind astray.

Between Us

At last, in the city garden, we meet again after what feels like ages. I walk towards you, briskly over the footbridge and through the hot, humid air, my arms eagerly extending outward for a hug. But when I come within a couple paces of you, I suddenly find myself hitting something and recoiling away from you. I stumble backwards, regaining my balance. Stunned, I look at you, seeing a rippling, transparent surface just in front of you, like a thin sheet of water. You're surprised too, your eyes meeting mine, full of puzzlement and concern.

Finally, as the ripples dissipate to leave no visible trace of anything between us, I ask, "What's with the wall?"

I watch your lips move, hearing nothing. You try to shout something, perhaps an explanation, but to no avail; your forcefully projected words seem to only mildly perturb the wall, ruffling it slightly. You shrug and motion at a nearby bench, then with slow, somber steps walk over to it.

You sit down, and I cautiously approach, my every step taken warily. I manage to sit beside you without incident.

"Can you hear me?" I ask.

You give me a puzzled look. The wall seems impervious to our voices. I wish I had something to write with. Your chest heaves with a silent sigh. Then you launch your fist in my direction, landing a punch upon a patch of the wall that lies before my face.

Your knuckles merely become the epicenter of a wave that slowly expands.

"Are you okay?" I ask.

You don't respond, but you don't look like you're in pain; you simply retract your hand and rest it upon your lap. I take out my pocket knife and poke at the wall. Little ripples form around the tip of the knife. Then, using both hands in a concerted effort to push the blade into the wall, I try to cut through it, but it's like trying to pierce ice.

You shake your head with disappointment, and I put away the knife. For a moment, I think about getting a hammer, then surmise that that probably won't do much either.

For a while we just sit there, watching the river flow westward, ducks bobbing on its surface.

Later, when the sun has slipped behind a cloud, I reach out my hand towards you to see if the wall is still there. I feel a cold surface that undulates as I press upon it. Feeling its otherwise featureless texture, I can't tell if the wall consists of sorrow, insecurity, jealousy or anger. Or for that matter whether it's coming from me or you or both of us. I withdraw my hand as you look on, disheartened.

Then, feeling tired, I lean my head against the barrier between us. I shiver as it chills my cheek, the sensation surprisingly refreshing in this summer heat. I imagine the wall suddenly dissolving and my head falling upon your shoulder.

As the Past Tries to Catch Up
With You: Part 5

As the colors of the sky thin, so do my ties with the people I've gotten to know here. With your company, I become socially myopic, my interpersonal field of view filled by our relationship. Because we regularly inhabit the same space and time, my social tendencies are prone to seeking their satiation from you, and I don't feel much desire to be around others. Though it's undoubtedly unhealthy, I can't help it. You quench my needs for human contact on a deep level.

With only a few exceptions, I decline invitations to get-togethers and only see colleagues, friends and acquaintances almost entirely by coincidence. When I happen to encounter members of the social scenes I now dismiss, I deflect inquiries about my absence with vague remarks about being busy. I take this decreased participation in the lives of people I know here as an indication of the tenuosity of my relationships with them and of the importance or at least immediacy of your presence.

Linguistically, there's no contest. You and I swap stories on a daily basis, about everything from happenings at work to the escapades of our once-mutual friends. These regular verbal transactions wholly supplant the social prattle once so prevalent during my days, eliminating those exchanges of insubstantial and innocuous remarks on pop-cultural trends and bouts of polite banter that have been quotidian fixtures of my interpersonal life. When it comes to mood, you're reliably a combination of contemplative calm and tempered vibrance, so I every now and then crave episodes of unrestrained enthusiasm or delirious alacrity, which I sometimes get at work from Risa.

Once a week or two, my already in-hibernation love life is unexpectedly and pleasantly prodded by warm conversations and charming smiles but never roused out of its deep slumber. Earlier in the year, the gradual but ultimately complete dissolution of my long-standing default crush on Virea left me romantically soporific, probably to both her benefit and mine.

Meanwhile, you become prone to wandering the city and visiting his favorite places, to be available to a chance encounter that might propel you towards him, to be accessible to the possibility that someone who knows him will find you familiar or even recognize you as his past self and strike up conversation. You become a slightly chatty presence in the jazz and singer-songwriter rooms of the music-sampling lounge, the cozy little juice bar and the artisan pizza place where the crust is a chewy canvas for the combinatorial arrangement of toppings like capers, sriracha sauce, chives, potato and chard.

You know from your skills and talents that vectors for the scenario trajectories you seek lie at the fringe of your plausibility spaces. But with nothing else to go on, you linger for hours in architectural design galleries, data studios, the oceanarium and soup cafés, studying the ambiance of their denizens, made nauseous by mind-numbing amounts of small talk that casting about for leads inevitably entails. You begin to lose confidence in your intuition as everything you try feels more and more like fruitless guesswork.

Some nights you come back as I'm getting ready for bed. You heat up leftovers from whatever dinner I've cooked, then silently conclude your day eating in the company of your thoughts. Sometimes we trade the words we're not too tired to give each other. I follow your lead, saving what I want to say for the next day if you don't say much.

Judging by the fatigue you often carry back with you, you're probably getting more than enough exercise while looking around the city for anything that vaguely resembles a clue. But when you need a different kind of workout, we go to the pool in the neighborhood school, one of the city's many gymnastics studios or the nearby vita course. You're not as into exercise as I am, not the fitness enthusiast I remember you being. You don't revel in intentional physical exertion the way you used to. Which makes sense considering how you're stingy with your time when it comes to activities that aren't related to finding him. It's like exercising with me is simply a way to maintain a healthy physique that will allow you to continue the pursuit, the rest of which is likely to be lengthy and difficult—lengthy because it'll be difficult.

I was easy to stalk. You'd know me by appearance even if my body mass index doubled, my hair turned frizzy brown and my wardrobe got overhauled by unruly fashionistas. You are very familiar with characteristics of mine not so easily changed: my eyes, posture and mannerism—for instance, the slight tilting my head to concentrate on something I'm looking at. And it was easy for you to figure out some of my favorite hangouts; his wall calendar chronicled all of our get-togethers with meeting time and location information, revealing our favorite cafés and parks in the city.

Finding his other friends, coworkers and acquaintances required more effort, but of course you rose to the challenge of locating and observing them, appetized by each piece of information you successfully gleaned in your sleuthing. But like me, they revealed nothing about his whereabouts, leaving you to try your luck around the city.

It's as though he has insulated parts of his psyche from the surrounding world with tactfully, even meticulously positioned solitude and privacy, to carefully sequester aspects of his life from us. It's not that he's made his life incomprehensible; he's left us uncomprehending of key facets of it.

I never knew him as well as I knew you. But knowledge isn't always required for a feeling of closeness.

Ciphers and Their Decoders

I hire a cryptologist to decipher your feelings. To me, they are utterly convoluted: a tangled jumble of incongruous and even contradictory emotions, but I'm certain that there's coherent, significant meaning encrypted in them. To her, this may merely be a heap of laundry that she'll wash, fold and sort. Her training is extensive, her career fledgling yet distinguished, so her code-cracking efforts should be well worth the hourly rate she charges.

"This is an interesting one," she tells me, assessing the conglomeration of emotional expression in my living room. "The encoding is all over the place. I doubt the cryptographer has the key. Oh, maybe he or she thinks he or she's got the key, but you know what he or she's probably got? *A dud*, that's what. But don't you worry. I'll get this decoded."

"Great," I reply, smiling. "Will it take a while? I mean, I'm just curious. There's no hurry."

"Yeah, could take a good while. Just do whatever you need to and check back later."

"Sounds good," I agree.

As I amble through meadow 5B on my way to the astrocognition lab, the warm, early-October air soothes my mind, eases my mental hold on the frustrations of failed attempts to extract your feelings from the amalgam of manifested emotions. I feel relaxed enough to gaze up into the sky, at the seemingly boundless pale magenta continuum punctuated now and then with its chartreuse clouds high up in the chromostrata.

But as I look at the expanse above, something feels off. I

stop in my tracks, and then I know exactly what it is. I see the clouds not as shapes corresponding to objects and animals but merely as… clouds—bodies of water vapor suspended in the atmosphere.

My eyes widen, then I blink at the sky in disbelief. The clouds haven't looked this way since I was a small child, before I learned to read clouds. I drop my gaze to the knee-high grass beside me, take a few deep breaths, and look up at the sky again, half hopeful that there's been some momentary… mistake. But when I return my gaze to the sky, it's still the same: the clouds don't look like wispy or puffy renditions of anything. They're just wisps and plumes. I continue staring at them, just in case it might take a while for them to appear as they usually do, for my mind to construe their forms as similar to things like cheese and dolphins. Nothing changes.

Unnerved, I continue walking, wondering what's going on. I've never heard of this happening to anyone, so could it be a rare condition or a bizarre symptom of fatigue?

I try to figure out how to appropriately respond. After some consideration, I decide to panic.

As I sit in the waiting area of my metaphysiologist's building, the receptionist kindly administers some chocolate, the pacifying effects of which make the waiting tolerable. So much so that I lapse into a short nap and have to be woken by the receptionist when my metaphysiologist is ready to see me.

I walk into her cozy office of bamboo flooring and walls of frosted glass. As is customary, I sit down on the red beanbag opposite her metallic-mesh one.

"Now, what seems to be the trouble?" she asks, looking at me intently with her violet eyes.

I describe my situation.

"Okay, well, have you noticed any other… changes?" she then asks.

"Not really, no."

"Has anything unusual or significant happened lately, before your altered perception of clouds?"

"Not really. Things have just been more mundane than they usually are."

"Okay, what about before that? Before this… dullness set in."

"Well, mostly I was… becoming versed in the art of bird-watching and techniques of beekeeping, up until the relevant seasonal changes took full effect."

"I see. Well, I think it would be best to run a few tests to further paint the painting we're painting here," she says.

Placing her hands firmly on the bamboo flooring, she pushes herself up from the beanbag, torso lifting steadily as her legs extend, baggy athleisure chinos swaying slightly.

She walks over to one of her office cabinets and removes some boxes, probably test kits. Returning to her beanbag, she places the boxes beside her, piled up in a short stack with the topmost box the smallest, a pack of playing cards; we used them the last time I was here.

"Let's try this one first," she says, opening the pack of playing cards, then laying them out facedown on the floor. "You're familiar with Concentration?"

I nod, and we begin flipping cards. Before long, she's leading by a wide margin. I make a modest comeback towards the end of the game, but it's too little too late.

"Interesting," she remarks while gathering up the cards. "Let's move on to some free association. You remember how this works, right?"

"Yup. You roll the dice, and I tell you what the resulting number evokes."

"Exactly."

She opens the box of assorted dice and lays out three ten-sided dice before her: pink, loud and plaid.

"We'll do double digits," she says. "Then triple, if necessary."

I nod. She rolls. The loud die clatters noisily upon the floor before being immobilized by gravity and friction to yield an 8. The pink one quietly but brightly results in a 3.

"Thirty eight," she tells me.

"The plush mountainside bungalow I stumbled upon while wandering mountains at the outskirts of the neighborhood I grew up in."

"Ah, your father, yes," she remarks, gathering up the dice.

She rolls again.

"Fifty five," she reads out.

"The taste of eggnog."

"Not your first taste or some specific kind of eggnog?"

"No, just eggnog generally."

"Fascinating," she whispers with a peculiar hoarseness, left eyebrow rising almost imperceptibly, like a twitch incompletely suppressed.

After the next roll, she tells me, "Thirty six."

"Feeling boxed in, between being cozy and constricted."

"Can you be more specific?"

"While growing up, as an elementary school child."

"Good, good. I think that's actually quite enough to go on," she concludes, putting away the dice.

I'm expectant of another test, perhaps the one where she lays out at random pictures of people, places and objects then asks me to construct a story with them. But she doesn't open any of the other boxes beside her.

"It looks like you're undergoing significant mental digestion and assimilation, to the extent that your mind is pushing out older, less useful mental processes to accommodate the new ones," she explains. "Likely all you've learned of birdwatching and beekeeping is being mentally metabolized."

"Why doesn't my mind just grow larger?"

"Grow into what? The psyche can't just expand to let its constituents enlarge."

"But surely there's still some space—some room to grow?"

"For pre-post-adolescents and more mature adults, mental space is made by the elimination of structures occupying regions of it and to some extent by the bundling and folding up of structures like conceptual knowledge. So you and I and those of similar maturity level have little choice but to lose the old in order to gain the new or let our thoughts and memories become compacted and convoluted."

"So this is normal?"

"Yes. That's partly why you don't have all the memories of your childhood that you once did. It's that automatic, selective, generally harmless amnesia ceaselessly at work in our lives."

"Wow."

"Let me give you a more intuitive example. Over time, have you been able to keep in your heart all the feelings you've had for people? Have you, for example, always cared for all your friends from high school with the same intensity since you knew them back then?"

"Well, no."

"Exactly. Our hearts *do not* have the capacity to retain all these feelings. When we come to have lofty affections or substantial admiration for someone, they often push out the more diminutive fondness we might have for others. A huge crush can shove feeble friendships and mild attractions to the periphery of the heart or the vast beyond."

"I see. But what about the exercises and activities one can

do to stimulate cardiac growth?"

"Those certainly increase cardiac capacity, but the heart can't grow to indefinite extent. With the heart and mind, this ebb and flow is almost constantly ongoing. It just comes down to whether you are aware of—experience the limitations. And now you are experiencing a manifestation of the human mind's limitations."

"So my situation is completely natural?"

"Yes, so far as we can tell."

"But what if I lose something more important than cloud reading, which I am pretty fond of actually."

"Oh, there's little danger in that. Some important memories and ideas might get pushed out, but much of what will go is trivial."

"And there's no way to choose what gets retained and what gets abandoned?"

"There are several ways to increase the chances of mental retention. Hypnosis or continual usage of specific mental processes, for example—those are fairly effective. Is there something in particular you want to hang on to?"

"I'd really like to hang on to certain memories and skills."

"Keep remembering those memories and using those skills. That should do it. If you find that ineffective, we'll set up a hypnosis session."

"Great. Thanks for your help," I reply, grateful that she's figured this all out and that there's a way to resist this dismantling of memory.

"Sure thing. Come back in a week or two for a followup, and we'll see how things are going with that mind of yours."

The walk home is uneventful. The sky looks strangely foreign to me, missing the intricacies I've become so accustomed to, the ever-changing meanings I could regularly see within it. Above me lies a once-familiar language I've lost literacy of.

When I get home, my living room feels surprisingly full of absence. The muddle of emotions is gone, replaced by a single sentiment.

There's a slip of paper on the kotatsu. It's the invoice for the deciphering work with a note that reads, "Do not be alarmed by the final outcome of the decryption. There was a lot of redundancy and noise in the code."

I sit down on the tatami, and despite my fatigue, I consider the resultant meaning of your emotions because they seem to gently demand my attention.

Sorry about all the lost time. Let's make the most of the moments we can still share.

Naïve Naturalism

Just minutes after getting back to my apartment from a stargazing session at the civic center planetarium, I get a phone call from you.

"Let's go hiking," you say right after I pick up.

"Okay," I answer, flopping on to my sofa. "When?"

"You got plans for tomorrow?"

"I was going to get some groceries, but I can do that later."

"Awesome, let's meet at the Thartles in the morning then."

"Okay."

For a moment, I think about the asymmetry of our mental perspectives. You can imagine me languid on this sofa or standing by the window that looks down the hill. You've been here and can guess at how I'm situated in this space. But I've never seen the apartment you call "home base" and have described as "perfect for conformatarians" and "an *emptimess* of material quandaries," cluttered with things yet lacking in meaning. I have no idea if you're stretched out on your own sofa beside windows with gaudy curtains or sitting at a small kitchen table that's home to little bottles of hot sauce.

"By the way, I was thinking about what we were talking about yesterday," you say. "What you were getting at, it seems like, is whether or not you should have faith in people. Faith that they will communicate with some level of honesty."

"I suppose that's it. Or a key aspect of it," I reply, considering your insight.

"I think that in urban areas, we may implicitly operate with that faith. Or maybe we need to have that faith. It's not like living in a small town or a farming village where people know or at least know of each other and are obviously interconnected and interdependent. Instead, we can be suspended in isolation, apparently untethered to each other because we have a system in which we're too often dependent on each other with specificity, anonymity and interchangeability.

"Like you were saying, you only know the barista as the barista. Getting our espresso from her, that's our only connection to her. And so long as someone makes espresso there, people can rest assured that they have at least one place to get good espresso. Since so many of our relationships are so limited, when we try to find out about all the other dimensions of someone's life, we have to have faith in their words. At least during conversations."

"Right, and that faith in people's words includes then faith in people's understanding of themselves."

"Yeah, we have to trust that they know themselves well enough so we can get a good sense of who they truly are from their own descriptions. I would say usually this faith is not misplaced and tends to be mutual."

"I definitely agree. It's just that, well, aren't there times when you want to know things for certain? Even seemingly trivial things, like is so-and-so's ex-girlfriend really *that* annoying or why did the sunset make him feel so old suddenly?"

"I know what you mean. But I think most of my interactions with people give me a satisfactory feeling of certainty."

"Well, I'm glad you feel that way."

When we meet at the north entrance to the Thartles, the weather is welcoming. It's as if the clear sky and warm breeze are the landscape promising us that the hiking will be excellent. And it's a promise that's easy to keep. We take the Nomilar

Trail up to a ridge that straddles grassy slopes speckled with wildflowers, ever enfolded by vibrant colors, like nothing is out of place here. When we stop to have lunch on a bench just off the dirt path, even the sandwiches we eat seem to be part of the ecology here—as though we are devouring pieces of the terrain and the very minutes that pass by.

Later, as we're on a descent into one of the valleys, we happen upon a friend of mine. Suddenly there she is standing in the middle of the trail, in the shadows of trees, drinking water when we round a sharp bend through a wooded patch.

"What are you doing here?" I ask as we stop just a few steps from her.

"Same thing you are," she says, capping her water bottle. "Hiking."

"I had no idea you come to this place," I remark.

"Yeah. I don't hike here very often, but I felt like coming here today," she says. "Which direction are you headed? I was planning to take the Muiv Valley Trail."

"Oh, same here," I reply.

"Can I join you?" she asks.

I turn to you before answering.

"I don't mind. It's totally up to you," you tell me.

"All right," I say. "Let's hike together then."

"Great!" she replies.

I'm about to introduce you to her, but she's quick to add, "Shall we get going?"

And you immediately answer, "Sure."

So all I can say is, "Okay," left with the impression that introductions are unnecessary, that you and she will get acquainted as we go.

The three of us get going at a pace that's both energetic and leisurely, quickly leaving behind the woods to walk upon a crest golden with dried grass. Then, as I look up into the vast arc of the sky, I notice that we're very quiet. Reticent, even. Perhaps we're each concerned about disrupting each others' communion with nature. Our silence is punctured only by occasional observations we share with each other. I spot a fox trotting down the hillside and point it out. You notice a few milfoil flowers, rare for this time of year. She names the birds she identifies by the songs she hears.

She doesn't try to strike up conversation with you, and you don't say anything to her. I'm a little surprised. You're not very talkative around people you aren't familiar with, but she usually is, adept at chitchatting with almost anyone. Maybe you two are both preoccupied soaking in the scenery or considering your own thoughts, but I sense an awkward ambiance about us, like there could be some tension among our personalities.

We enter a wooded, gently ascending trail and follow it along a narrow canyon lushly lined with shrubs and small trees.

"Reminds me of the wildlife refuge in that film *Vanity's Lair*," I muse aloud. "Like we're walking through one of the scenes."

"Yeah, the vegetation is pretty similar," you agree.

"I haven't seen that film yet," she says.

"Oh, you've *got to*," you exclaim. "Nearly every scene is exquisitely framed."

"I should make it a point watch it soon. I've been meaning to for the longest time," she says.

Then, for almost the entire length of this canyon, we walk without any further conversation until we meet a man walking in the direction opposite us.

He slows from his brisk pace as he nears us, then pauses a couple steps in front of us to ask, "Do you happen to know if we're close to the north entrance?"

As the three of us come to a stop, she says quickly, "Sort of," before you or I can reply.

"Just keep going the way you're headed until you intersect Rurz Way. Then take a left and follow Rurz to Nomilar. Then take a right, and it's just a short distance to the entrance," she explains.

"Great, thanks a lot," he says.

"No problem," she says.

"Well, enjoy the beautiful weather," he says.

"Thanks," you reply, smiling.

"You too," I add.

He continues on his way, and we continue on ours.

"For someone who doesn't come here often, you're pretty familiar with the trails," I say to her.

"Oh, I took those last time," she replies.

After ascending the last hill on the final leg of our trek, we sit down at a small wooden picnic table. You sit beside her, opposite me. Quietly, we each stare out upon the landscape, eating granola bars and drinking water from her metal water bottle. The sky feels distinctly autumnal in hue.

But the vast scenery of golden hills and tangles of wispy clouds doesn't hold my attention for long. The silence among us soon becomes the most obvious element of the atmosphere here. The reticence that has enveloped us this entire hike alludes to disquieting possibilities. Finally, I become overwhelmed by the need to deal directly with it, with the dynamic among us.

"Not feeling talkative today?" I ask her.

She gives me a look of incredulity and says, "I thought you weren't feeling talkative."

"Oh, really?"

"Honestly, I was starting to feel like you wanted more solitude and that I was imposing on your hike and you were too nice to say no," she says.

"More solitude?" I echo, baffled. Did she mean privacy?

"Yeah, I thought you might be one of those people who prefers to hike alone," she elaborates.

Alone? My eyes dart to you, and you give me a look of confusion and shrug. My eyes return to her.

"I'm going to ask you a question that might be a little strange," I begin uncertainly. "But I want you to answer it truthfully, okay?"

"Well, okay," she says, a little taken aback by the words I've suddenly sprung upon her.

"Is there someone sitting next to you?" I ask.

She regards me skeptically and answers, "*Next to me?* No."

"*What?*" you blurt, then shout, "I'm right here."

"Has it been just the two of us walking and talking so far this afternoon?" I ask.

She says immediately, "Aside from the man who asked for directions, yes."

My eyes flit to meet yours, which gaze intently at me.

"She's lying," you say to me. "She must be messing with you by not paying attention to me," you add vehemently.

Emphatically you wave your right hand in front of her face, but she doesn't react in even the slightest way. So you place your hands firmly on her shoulders and shake her vigorously. I watch her torso rock back and forth as you do this, but she seems to remain oblivious to the movement you've imposed upon her. Her expression remains unchanged. I stare blankly at this befuddling scene.

You let go of her, and she asks me, "Are you feeling okay?"

"She's probably slightly psychotic or jealous of me," you conjecture, perhaps in hopes of provoking her to acknowledge you.

She simply awaits my answer.

After a very awkward descent to the east gate, we stand

on the gravel road into the Thartles, by the threshold between rustic and suburban environments.

"Want to go get a beer and snacks?" she asks, pointing to the street of shops and eateries just outside the gate.

"Next time. I think there's something I should take care of," I tell her as I look at you.

"Right now?" she asks, a little startled.

"Yes, well, as soon as possible. It's sort of personal," I say vaguely and add, "I'll treat you to beer and something next time."

"Well, okay then," she says. "See you at the Workshop."

"Yes, see you there," I answer distractedly.

She heads out the gate, leaving the two of us lingering here. "Let's go to your apartment," I suggest.

"What, now?" you blurt. "It's going to take over an hour to get over there, and it's really messy at the moment."

"I don't mind. I just want to see where you live."

You're quiet with hesitation.

"Please," I implore. "If I can know with more certainty that you actually live somewhere, I'll feel less crazy."

"Don't you trust me?"

"I want to. Maybe I don't trust myself."

You sigh and say with a faint smile, "All right, let's go."

Preoccupied, I barely hear the clatter of the moving train. I try to remember if I have ever seen you change the world in a way that has conclusive, definite reality.

"I'm not some fabrication of your psyche," you protest as if responding to the blur of thoughts in my mind. "You can talk with my parents on the phone, or I can show you my voter registration receipt."

"I'm not sure what would prove anything," I lament.

"For all we know, she could be the imaginary one," you toss out almost wildly.

I shake my head and reply, "No, that can't be right. If she's imaginary and you're not, there's no way you could perceive her. And she gave directions to that man."

"That doesn't mean anything. You could be imagining all of us. You could have given directions to that man and imagined it was her."

I consider this.

"It seems to me," you continue. "Your mind could come up with a variety of ways to make something—almost anything— seem real. What's to stop you from hallucinating the small, squalid apartment I live in? In fact, you can never truly know what's actually real or if there's even a world beyond that which your mind has put together. It's just a question of consistency. We all just interpret what's consistent with everything else to be reality."

"That's true," I murmur.

My gaze wanders out the window beside me. We're passing by a schoolyard. For an instant, I see groups of high school students in athletic uniforms. Then we're crossing a river where a few herons stand in the shallow waters. For all I know, the students and birds could be sheer fabrications of mind. They might as well be. Few if any of them will ever do anything that will affect me directly. This is perhaps only marginally different from seeing dragons flying in the sky. Then again, aren't the cumulative effects of many direct and indirect consequences constantly influencing our lives? Isn't that quintessential to the structure of our personal circumstances and reality at large?

But maybe my very conception of the world has been based upon subtly but fundamentally inaccurate assumptions. I start to wonder if reality isn't a continuum but a collection of discreet pieces, not all of which are in causal contact with each other.

"Maybe then whatever any of us are, we should try to interact with each other respectfully and meaningfully," I venture.

You nod and reply, "Yeah, that makes sense to me," then after a brief pause add, "You still want to go to my apartment?"

"Well, we're already on our way there."

"Okay, that's cool. But I think it will disappoint you in at least one way."

That's fine with me. If disappointment is the price of knowing its unequivocal realness, I'll gladly pay.

As the Past Tries to Catch Up
With You: Part 6

When late-autumn spells of white noise permeate our urban landscape, we talk only when the apartment windows are shut tight or while visiting well-insulated indoor venues. We get into a habit of verbally communicating only episodically when the ambient static is held at bay (to varying degrees of success) by human-made barriers. It's that solitary time of year when people spend more time with their own thoughts, when voices and traffic are effortlessly muffled beneath the low hiss that fills the air, that hushed gushing which can so easily lull us into daydreams and sleep, especially after lunch. Many city dwellers can be seen in cafés, libraries and parks reading novels, writing in diaries, drawing in sketchbooks or pumping music into their ear canals with headphones. Even the city's most frenetic neighborhoods are overcome with an uncanny calm.

Unaccustomed to this aspect of life here, you're initially disoriented, thrown by people's reluctance to converse, by their more introspective moods. Their reticence leads you to feel isolated—not that you've become that connected to people here, but your default identity as a newcomer and outsider seems only amplified.

During this annual period of white noise, we go about our lives seemingly withdrawn. We still crave verbal communion, but the desire to engage each other is diminished by the white noise, which makes our voices less comprehensible, to the extent that ambiguity is averted only with loud, emphatic articulation or full-on shouting—an amount of effort that discourages small talk. This time of the year vies with the depths of winter for the distinction of being the loneliest season. To you, this is more disconcerting than winter. Instead of freezing temperatures and snow keeping us indoors and separated from each other, our daily routines continue to bring us into shared spaces and close proximity, but our behavior is modified to obviate discussion as much as possible.

At work, there is a dearth of our usually abundant chitchat in the labs, lounges and hallways. Only nods and smiles are exchanged in passing. The hiss that hangs upon the city streets seeps into the old building we occupy, its poor insulation insufficient for maintaining a noise-free interior. The amount of time we spend composing and perusing memos at least doubles. We hear each other's voices almost exclusively in the conference room, which has been outfitted with a filter to reduce ambient white noise.

The subdued, almost somber ambiance can both soothe and suffocate the psyche. This is exactly what it does to you.

The seasonal conditions leave your mind abundant time and mental wherewithal to contemplate your future self, to mull over the varied minutiae you've uncovered of his life here, for anything that could be a lead. You appreciate this expanded ability to focus on the long-stalled pursuit, but this enabling of your obsessive quest puts you at risk of bearing more disappointment and pressure.

I wish you were like most of our fellow city dwellers during this time of year. I've heard they go to bed early and sleep more soundly with the white noise.

During these evenings when the sonic fuzz obscures the creaking of the floorboards underfoot, I approach whatever room you're in, then hover at its edge and let my gaze rest upon you.

Often you're sitting on the living room floor composing disparate ideas into coherent thoughts. As your hands and eyes work deftly, it is as if I am just outside the bubble of space and time that is yours alone, the region only your consciousness can occupy. And it's there that the solitary nature of human existence becomes very nearly tangible, that despite the intimacy of our interactions with each other and our selves, our experiential essences can only border one another.

When the ambient hissing has dissipated, we go for an afternoon outing to enjoy the aurally crisp air. We end up at the outskirts of the city, where we rent a canoe from a recreation stand on the riverbank. Undulating nostalgically beside us, the water flows at a pace that seems to match that of our thoughts. With rhythmic unhurriedness we dip our canoe paddles into the water, push some force into it, and lift the paddles back into the air.

"Who did you miss most when you moved away?" you ask, quietly and slowly, like the overcast sky has set the tone for the conversation you're starting.

"I missed all of you in different ways, but for a long time, I really wanted to talk with Haruhi," I answer, still finding it a little strange conversing while facing your back.

"Somehow I thought so," you remark. "That it would be Haruhi. That you'd miss her like an insomniac yearning for lyrical dreams."

"Yeah, it wasn't as intense as that, but there's a whole swath of time that's tinged with a longing to have conversations with her," I add.

"So what did you do all those times you wanted to talk with her?"

"Mostly I wrote letters. Some of which I never sent."

"Why?"

"They were embarrassing. Incriminating, really."

"Of what?"

"Of emotional robbery—this city's theft of my confidence and convictions by my new surroundings. The majority of the unsent letters were too verbose in a way that was thoroughly revealing of my anxieties and insecurities."

"I never thought you'd feel that way about Haruhi."

"Well, ordinarily I wouldn't have, but you have to understand, I had just left everything and everyone that I'd been connected with for years, and in the struggle to form new connections, doubts began to infiltrate my views of the world. They'd end up in my letters to Haruhi more often than I should have allowed."

"I'm sure she understood that you were in a situation that made you psychologically vulnerable."

"Right, but I didn't want to impose the effects of that vulnerability upon her too frequently. I didn't want it to dominate our correspondence."

"I see."

Then we simply continue to paddle until you ask, "Do you still have those letters?"

"I'm sure I do. Squirreled away somewhere."

"Can I read them sometime?" you ask, then add, "To get to know you a little better. And maybe him too."

The second part of what you've said doesn't make sense to me. Then it does.

A week later, flocks of violet-winged lullaby jays transit the swath of sky above the city. As they start their annual journey north, their individually soothing voices amalgamate into a squealing avian cacophony telling us that autumn is drawing to an end. You are mesmerized by the awesome abundance they manifest multiple times a day.

We spend the majority of a Thursday afternoon gazing out the windows of the library observatory as droves of innumerable birds with purple and grey plumage pass over the city. We hadn't meant to watch them for so long. I came to compile the latest articles on cognitive autoimmunity. You came to find information about some of his clients, hoping that you might uncover a clue to his whereabouts. You're probing for scenarios that span a range of likelihoods.

At the probable end of the spectrum are scenarios that go something like: he fell into favor with a client tied to a network of community influence that your future self then tapped into to make arrangements for travel and the obfuscation of his movements. A fair distance from these sorts of scenarios, there are ones tinged with various shades of dubiousness—ones that might go along the lines of: a client happens to describe her obscure but delightfully rustic hometown to him, piquing his attention to the extent that he later visits the place on a whim; the local culture of farming and crafts is thoroughly captivating, and the real estate there is alluringly affordable, so much so that he impulsively yet secretively purchases a bungalow that he can use for vacations or to hide from you.

In the library, we each embarked upon our respective research, but it wasn't long before we glanced out the windows and saw the jays streaking across the sky in dense masses. Once we had glimpsed that, we had to go up to the observatory for a better look, certain that we'd be satisfied with just a few minutes there. But we're still here, sitting in plastic chairs with our attention in the clutches of this avian spectacle before us.

"There are that many in this region?" you murmur, lost in wonderment.

"Yes. Tracts of forest full of them," I reply, in a hushed voice.

"It's a staggering reminder that nature deals in multitudes."

"While we tend to deal in singularities?"

"I suppose in conscious cognition there can be that tendency," you reply, turning your attention from the flocks to me. "Unless you're doing something that involves larger scales. Like politics or manufacturing."

"Ah, that reminds me of the tree bank. That stands out to me as an example of something operating at a large scale that we understand at a much smaller scale—the scale of our involvement."

"Right. They must manage millions of people's arboreal assets in the form of various seeds, saplings and trees, but we think of it in the oversimplified terms that are most relevant to us: deposit a seed or sapling, make regular payments to tend the growing tree, withdraw the tree when you want it."

"Yeah, that's still my picture of how it works," I reply, briefly seeing in my mind's eye this simplistic representation once again. "I've never seen where they keep all the trees and have no conception of the sheer volume of assets they maintain."

"I bet their facilities are mind-blowingly vast. Not only do they need space for all the growing trees and seeds, but they also need the resources to take care of them. Their soil design and testing labs alone must be huge. It's amazing that the affordable upkeep fees they charge cover all their operations."

"It is impressive," I agree.

"Speaking of fees, do you pay yours by mail? Wait, do you even still have an account with them?"

"No. When I left, I wasn't sure when or if I'd have a place for trees, so I turned my account over to Haruhi so she could have the trees later or donate them."

"She didn't mind the additional expense?"

"Not at all. She was happy to take on the assets since the deposits I made diversified her account with more deciduous trees. They'll also give her more older, larger trees in the future."

"Oh, right. I forgot how much Haruhi likes evergreens."

"Yeah, bare branches evoke a sense of emptiness in her," I add, recalling the toll winter walks through the woods could take on her.

"Ah, and that brings up another aspect of the tree bank that's interesting too. Over time, you're depositing seeds, seedlings and saplings with the expectation that they will grow into trees that a future self of yours will plant somewhere," you say quickly in that epiphanal tone of voice. "You're probably putting in trees you like, that you assume your future selves will like. And a lot of times, you do pass on your tastes to future selves, but there are definitely times when we don't. I'm sure some future selves end up liking trees that are very different from the trees their past selves loved dearly."

"No doubt," I agree. "It's highly plausible that someone would end up annoyed that her or his past self deposited so many oaks, for example."

"Exactly. Maybe a future Haruhi will end up thinking, 'I'm so glad I got that infusion of deciduous. Having just the firs would've been monotonous.' Giving her your account could safeguard against future dissatisfaction with past preferences."

"I hadn't thought of that before, but you're right. There's that tendency we have to plan things out for our future selves based on what we think they will need and like, which is tied, perhaps inextricably, to what we need and like. But we know now how different our selves can be from each other."

As soon as I've said this, I'm afraid I've gone too deep into the already touchy subject of future selves we've begun wandering.

"But that's all one can do as a present self: try to anticipate the wants and needs of future selves to the reasonable extent that one can," you reply, conversational enthusiasm clearly waning.

No, there's at least a little more one can do. But I don't think this is a good time and place to attempt the overturn of your beliefs. So I nod, and we continue gazing at the unending flux of birds obscuring sky and city.

Tension and Resonance

While we're taking a break from watering the plants of the rooftop garden, you ask me, "Don't you feel... something?"

Your voice is quieter than usual.

The awesome sweep of the geometrically grey cityscape distracts me, delays my answer. With our arms pressed upon the parapet, it's just us and this marvel of human engineering— the vast swath of urban landscape that makes the bright sky look drab in its comparative simplicity.

"Besides the breeze and warm humidity?" I ask, not sure what you mean.

"I mean *this*," you tell me, and then faintly I feel a tug on my psyche.

"Oh, I meant to tell you, I got my heart restrung. The old strings were fraying, and I was afraid they'd snap," I explain. "But the new ones are still stiff and haven't been tuned, so there isn't much of the usual sensitivity and resonance."

Considering this, your lips press together tightly, then you nod slightly.

"Okay," you say at last with what sounds like relief to my less responsive heart. "No wonder you've been pretty aloof lately. I thought maybe you were ignoring me."

"No, I wouldn't do that. I just haven't made the necessary adjustments yet. It's kind of involved."

Something doesn't quite feel right about that explanation, so I add, "Sorry about that," in a tone of voice that ends up being awkward.

"No worries. Stiff strings are definitely better than broken ones."

I nod, and we lapse into silence and stare out at the myriad buildings forming neighborhoods and districts, the cliques of our city.

You turn around to lean your back upon the parapet, then say, "This makes me think of the time I became scared of pulling on my mom's heart strings."

"I didn't know you ever felt that way."

"Yeah, I don't talk about it much. But now I pretty much have to tell you the story since I've mentioned it."

"Well, if you'd rather not—"

"No, no. It would do me some good to talk about it."

"Okay."

You take a deep breath, then begin.

"One day after school when I was five or six, I really wanted some macaroni and cheese—my favorite afternoon snack. So I asked my mom to fix some up. She said very quietly that she would make me a bowl of it soon and told me I should draw some pictures while I waited.

"But after I had leisurely drawn four pictures on the living room coffee table, she was still lying on the sofa behind me. Not really thinking anything of it, I ended up doing what I often did back then: pull on her heartstrings a little. But she didn't react with her usual attentiveness, so I pulled a bit more insistently, and she suddenly yelled, 'Stop yanking on Mommy's heartstrings!' I was so shocked by the alien ferocity of her words that I let go immediately."

"Wow," I murmur, not sure what to make of what you've described; it has no counterpart in my childhood, and you usually talk so fondly of your mother.

"Then I must have shrunk back, because suddenly my mom looked further away from me, but don't remember moving. I must not have felt my body recoil. All I felt was scared that she might get physical."

"Like hit you?" I ask, more curious than appalled.

"More like throw or break something. She was looking at me with wide, glaring eyes. She seemed like someone else. Then she rushed out of the living room and into her bedroom. Not knowing what else to do, I just stared out the window for a while, watching the tree branches sway in the wind.

"But when my mom didn't come out of her room after what felt like the longest time I had ever waited for her, I became... not exactly concerned but curious. So I went to her room really quietly and looked through the keyhole. She was sitting on the bed with her back to me, but from her slouching posture, I was sure she was crying quietly. I hadn't really seen her cry before, but I just knew she was crying. You know how you can just tell?"

"Yeah."

"And that, in a way even more powerful than her words, made me very wary of touching her heart. Even now, I sometimes think twice before reaching out to her."

Despite my new heartstrings being unattuned to these sorts of moments, your story stirs them a little. I place my hand on your shoulder.

"But right now," you say, tilting your head to look up into the sky. "I could pull all I want on your heartstrings to barely any effect."

"You should pull all you want," I tell you, almost gruffly, like it's a dare.

"To loosen things up?" you infer tentatively, quietly.

I concentrate on modulating my tone, on getting the dampened, distorted emotions to resonate adequately with my voice.

"Yes, but also that will remind me you're really, actually here.

And that I am too."

As your lips stretch into a smile, your face brightens, as if the long shadow cast by your mother's outburst is ebbing.

Habits of Mental Hygiene

Before I know it, the price of mind cleanser is rising melodramatically, ascending like a manic mountaineer. Whenever the price dips—as if about to swoon, collapse in sheer fatigue from its rise to lofty heights—it then defies logic and expectations by leaping wildly, incredulously scrambling upward to stupefying exorbitance. Supposedly this frenetic activity is due to a sudden and increasing scarcity of the key ingredient: silence.

The upwardly lurching cost forces me to ration my remaining supply, to clear my mind only once every several days instead of several times everyday as I've usually done. The new routine of reduced refreshing that I'm trying to establish leaves my mind feeling cluttered and fettered with ideas and thoughts like never before, until I can at last revitalize my mind with the bit of cleanser I've allotted myself.

With my mind occupied and hampered for long periods of time, I become sluggish, the ever-increasing contents of my consciousness cumbersome, making mental activity difficult. I'll be attempting to put together a new understanding, expand upon an aspiration or organize some thoughts, only to have myriad other ideas interfere, distract me with their persistent presence, salience and sometimes gaudy jargon. Everything from conversation with friends to deliberation on personal matters becomes effortful to the point of being frustrating. It took me the better portion of last night to compose a short letter to Xire. I had to go to the kitchen three times this morning before finally getting the tangerines I wanted to bring with me to the studio.

After a week of struggling with an all-too-often fully occupied mind, I am in dire need of your advice, which I solicit while we're having some yogurt in the workshop cafeteria.

"I don't know how you do it," I tell you, pushing away fragments of gossip, work-related concerns and bits of fashionable triviality that could so easily slip into our conversation. "How is it that through all these years, you've been able to use mind cleanser so sparingly?"

"Because only rarely do I need it," you answer with a highly enviable composure; I haven't had anything like that since early yesterday morning.

"How is that possible with all the events going on around us and all the ideas going on within us? Not to mention all the mental activities that are demanded of us, let alone the mental activities we want to engage in?" I ask hurriedly, before these questions I've assembled in my mind are unraveled under the incessant bombardment of ideas floating around.

"Reduce, focus and displace," you answer with a matter-of-fact delight. "Reduce your exposure to ideas, especially sticky ones that are of little consequence to you. Focus on mental activities that don't produce clutter—or even better, activities that reduce clutter, that rearrange, combine or break down ideas into more manageable forms. Displace ideas and thoughts that muddle your mind by engaging ideas and experiences that are truly meaningful to you."

"Really? That works?" I ask, shoving aside song lyrics, economics statistics, and recounts of Xona's romantic escapades so I can keep in mind what you're saying.

"Yup, if you're diligent about having those kinds of habits. It becomes second nature after a while."

"So is there any way I can start doing any of those now?" I ask, desperate for some clarity of mind.

"Sure. Look me in the eyes—*really look*—and don't say anything."

Peering at your irises and pupils, I become ever more aware of the jumbled thoughts weighing on my mind. Worried that it's not working, that I'm doing this wrong, wanting to break off the eye contact that's becoming awkward, I struggle to hold my gaze steady.

Then slowly, your eyes take on a marvelous sense of depth. Miscellaneous details and factoids, anxieties and errands, social obligations and financial concerns drain from my mind. The world seems to go quiet as the connection of our gazes solidifies, locking us together in a moment of clarity.

Relentlessly Preemptive

While we're out on our forestwatching break, I can't stop my gaze from drifting to your chest. Something's there, beneath your baggy, sea-green plaid shirt. Trying to be discreet about it, I steal every glance I can, hoping to figure out what might be protruding from your chest, right around your heart.

Then, when you raise your arms up to stretch, the answer becomes apparent to me. As your shirt is pulled slightly upwards, I can make out the contours of three thin, shallowly jutting rods. They can only be the remains of arrow shafts. And judging by their stiffness, their integrity, they're still new, freshly cut stumps of metaphysical projectiles whose tips remain lodged in your heart.

But why are there three? One is usually more than enough.

I think this over, reviewing what I know. You've been thrice struck, yet you seem completely fine. Like nothing's happened. No dreamy gaze, no buoyant commentary on life, no euphoric, out-of-context smiles. This leads me to surmise that somehow, you must be refusing to fall in love, and perhaps Cupid is trying to combat your stubbornness. Is that it?

You haven't even vaguely hinted at the emotional fight you're waging, so it must be a matter you want to keep private. With that thought, I move my gaze back to the lanky birch trees before me.

At lunchtime, a moment after I sit down beside you at our usual cafeteria table, you remove a small bottle of blue pills from the tote bag you always carry. Quickly and nonchalantly, you open the bottle, shake a single pill out on to the palm of your left hand, and pop it into your mouth. After closing up the bottle and tucking it back into your bag, you swallow the pill with a swig of mango juice.

You do this so casually that I figure you've simply begun taking vitamins or some other dietary supplement, but somehow, I feel like I should show some concern, in case this is medication for some malady that's afflicting you.

"Everything okay?" I ask.

"Oh yeah, yeah. Completely fine," you tell me, nodding.

"Okay, that's good," I reply.

And we leave it at that.

Until after a few minutes of silent lunching have elapsed.

"You saw them, didn't you?" you whisper to me.

I put down my fork and turn my attention from the eggplant casserole to you. Not sure how to reply, I wave a hand vaguely at your chest.

You nod.

"All right," you say, as if coming to some crucial conclusion or decision in your mind. "I'll tell you what's going on. Later. Come over tonight."

Having no plans for the evening, I nod in agreement.

The early afternoon passes as it often does: nitty, gritty R&D business. Our team goes over the data we've collected to determine how much the latest thought-thinning agents we've developed reduce the viscosity of cognition, how much they allow big and small ideas to circulate about the mind. While we carry out the calculations, your focus doesn't waver for an instant. You manifest not even the slightest symptoms of being in love—no absentminded smile, no gazing off into space, no sporadic episodes of unfounded optimism. You're fervently constructing equations with Xire, formulating mathematical models of cognitive flow with exceptional zeal.

During today's afternoon colloquium, you're engrossed, listening keenly to the speaker describe his research on tuning emotional intensities. You frenetically scribble notes and pose the occasional thoughtful question. Afterwards, when I catch glimpses of you in solitary moments at your desk, you're poring over reports, then sketching out new experimental systems. If your attention has any propensity to wander, it's exceedingly infrequent and short-lived.

It's like you're in the clutches of another kind of love.

When I get restless a couple hours later, I walk around the institute and stop by the Chronition Department.

"Is Rurt in?" I ask one of her colleagues.

"Yeah, try the simulator room," he suggests.

"Okay, thanks."

And sure enough, Rurt is there, programming a new scenario with her cognisphere glowing all around her. Noticing me enter the room, she pauses in her work, and the holographic interface surrounding her dims.

Meeting my eyes with her intense emerald ones, she asks, "What's up?"

"Suppose someone were struck by two of Cupid's arrows, the second within several days of the first. How would that person feel?" I ask.

"Well, you know what just one can do," Rurt begins. "And the effects of love on people tend to be nonlinear, so a double dose of love could result in anything from delirious infatuation to incapacitation."

"Could anything weaken the effects?"

"Yeah, a number of things. Cogent rationality, meditation,

stress, sleep deprivation, the side effects of certain drugs. But the extent to which they'll decrease the intensity of love varies, depending on a range of factors."

"Okay," I murmur, wondering if I should ask Rurt what being struck by three arrows would be like.

"Did you need more specific information?" she asks, her eyes disengaging from mine, returning to the summary of scenario parameters floating to her left.

"No, just curious."

"All right. Well, if you want to talk more about this or other hypotheticals, I'll be getting some coffee in about half an hour in the cafeteria."

"Maybe I'll look for you there, but this has already been really helpful."

"Glad to be of assistance," Rurt says with a distracted smile.

Preoccupied by her work, she doesn't appear to give my questions any further thought.

Your place is, as always, dimly lit, making the chirping of crickets particularly loud as it seeps in through slivers of open window. The atmosphere feels strangely secretive, even paranoid. We sit on the tatami floor by your kotatsu. You pour the tea you've brewed for us. Its floral scent builds an atmosphere of cozy confidentiality.

"I knew I should have cut the shafts further down," you begin, placing the teapot between our teacups on the kotatsu. "But the closer to the arrowhead you handle the shaft, the more it aggravates the wound. At least it seems like you're the only person who's noticed so far."

"Why are there three?" I can't stop myself from asking. "How is it that one isn't enough?"

You point to the bottle of blue pills at the far end of the

kotatsu.

"Even four or five probably won't be enough," you tell me. "I've formulated an antidote."

All I can do is stare at you for a while, then finally ask, "So the arrows have no effect on you?"

"Well, they still sting. But as far as instigating romantic feelings goes, they're as effective as lemon juice is for remedying receding hairlines."

"So why don't you want to fall in love?"

"A while ago I determined that there's no one here I should fall in love with. Based on the psychological profiling analyses I've done, falling in love with anyone I know would be something between distraction and disaster. To put it simply, falling in love would be a mistake. So I started taking the antidote as a preventative measure."

"But romantic love isn't something you can treat with that kind of logic, and it changes people," I protest. "And what about people you don't know? You might meet someone fantastic just serendipitously."

"I'd rather wait for someone else to make the first move. Then, once I've gotten to know that person, I'll assess our compatibility, and if we're a good match for each other, I'll stop taking the antidote."

"You know he won't give up. He works for Fate."

"Yeah, but because he works for Fate, he's too busy to do anything but fire more arrows at me," you reply confidently. "So unless he can deprive me of the antidote—which I can always make more of—he's fighting an uphill battle. The only really likely scenario that will tip the situation in his favor is me forgetting to take the antidote. I have to swallow a pill roughly every six hours to make sure the doses of love from the time-release arrowheads are safely neutralized. But I've set alarms to remind me to take my pills."

"So who's the would-be object of your nullified affections?"

"I have no idea. To be as effective as possible, the antidote must preemptively neutralize any romantic feelings in their entirety. Not even the slightest inkling is left."

"You're not even a little curious who it might be?"

"Sure I'm curious. I'm also curious about spelunking, deep-sea exploration, bungee jumping and time travel. But now's not the time for any of those things."

"You might be missing something wonderful."

"I'll take that chance. I'm already in the midst of something truly wonderful," you tell me with a grin.

We lapse into a very comfortable silence. I admire your dedication to your values and vision for your life. You know with uncanny clarity what you want and have acted decisively.

Then, almost simultaneously, we take up our still-steaming cups from the kotatsu and sip the warm, fragrant tea within them.

A thought occurs to me, about what you said earlier about someone else making the first move. What if this was a case of mutual love at first sight or something like that? What if it was meant to be requited? That would mean you've turned this into a case of unrequited love. Is that why Cupid has been persistent and come back to strike you again and again? With this train of thought, I go from admiration to speculative sympathy, feeling sorry for a hypothetical third party—someone out there who may be anywhere from intrigued by to totally hung up on you, someone who looks at you longingly but is too shy to say anything.

There's a twinge in the cockles of my heart. I take another sip of tea to distract myself from the feeling. And it seems to just melt away.

Impending Invisibility

Slowly but unmistakably, I am forgetting you. And now, as we sit on a small swath of grass in the city's riverside gardens, I have to tell you what by all indications is irrevocably becoming my reality: a world in which you will no longer exist as you.

"Why is it *just me*?" you demand. "Am I so… unmemorable?"

"No, it's not that," I answer.

It's difficult for me to face you. I look at the maple trees, their foliage tipped with orange, like they are being slowly ignited into a vibrance that will be in full blaze next week.

"I used to remember you so well," I continue. "And a lot of other people remember you just fine."

"Well, if it's not me, and it's not you, it's like the universe can't just let us lead our lives. It has to throw us this curveball instead."

I'm not surprised that you're upset. I'm surprised you're not more upset.

I've been forgetting you for some time, but we've tried not to make too much fuss out of it. At times, we even managed to make light of it. But that was when it was far more benign—manifesting as odd absurdities that could humor us by suddenly and ridiculously overturning our long-held mutual understanding of each other. A few months ago, I gave you a portable professional persona for your birthday, the exact same birthday present I gave you three years ago. Then at a karaoke get-together a couple weeks later, I sang that song you just can't stand, which I can no longer remember the title of—I just remember you groaning, making gagging gestures at the lyrics I thought I was doing a good job on. With a little effort, these episodes became laughable.

It's gotten much worse lately. You have to keep reminding me of your political views, of your dearly held accomplishments and aspirations, of how we met, that you're allergic to artificial cherry flavoring, that you have a cat, that you were once a prodigy. It's like my conception of you is being hollowed out, relentlessly deprived of detail.

"So at this rate, soon I'll be just a total stranger to you," you conclude dismally, gaze directed at a lone heron standing on the riverbank. "And it doesn't seem like you're going to ever remember me again."

"That is the way it's going," I reluctantly agree.

"It's so unfair," you say. "I'll be the only one left remembering us—who we've been together, the roles we've played in each other's lives."

"Sadly, we don't get to decide how this goes. If I could pick a person who I had to forget, it'd be someone like Werna instead," I reply, hoping the last part will add a dash of levity.

A small smile flickers upon your face. I wait and watch long enough to know it's not coming back.

So I return to the serious tone of our conversation and tell you, "I can't choose to remember you any more than you can choose to forget me. If it were volitional, I'd do everything I can to remember you."

"I know."

You sigh. I don't know what to say. Maybe I don't remember enough to respond appropriately, to figure out the words that might help us through this.

"Well, maybe it could work out kind of okay this way," you say in a tentative tone. "In the future, whenever we see each other and end up talking or something, you'll be thinking, 'Oh, that's really nice this stranger is being so friendly to me.' If I don't explain the situation to you, that is."

"Would you really be all right with that? It does seem unfair, like you said."

"At least we can still hang out. It's not like we're going to be in different countries."

"I guess we can try that out. If it ends up upsetting you, just stop doing it," I tell you. "If you do, I won't know what I'm missing."

"All right. That makes sense."

Then I can't help but ask, "Do you think it would be better if we were in different countries or could never meet again but could still remember each other?"

"I don't know. Seems like these situations are each painful in their own ways."

I nod, reluctant to tell you that soon there will be no pain for me. When the final wisp of you in my thoughts dissolves, it will happen silently and unobtrusively, all knowledge of you gone like my dreams that dissolve completely upon waking and leave no traces in my consciousness. I won't know that anything has changed. But to you, the irrevocable shift will be obvious and poignant.

I look at your face, trying to be conscious of the nuances while they still have some intimate meaning to me. There's no way to know how much I once saw in your expressions and heard in your voice—anything I've forgotten and never told you is now lost to us.

But maybe then our moments together become chances to rediscover aspects of you, of us together—albeit ephemerally. So maybe I should tell you what I've found or fleetingly reclaimed in case I didn't before.

"You have a way of imbuing these silences between us with a sublime calm, even in moments like this," I say to you. "But I've probably said that already."

"No, you haven't. And even if you had, I wouldn't mind hearing it again."

You smile faintly, with a warmth still familiar to me, one which seems to reach deep into my heart, and I become certain that whatever happens, these smiles of yours will still touch my heart in some way.

At Each Other's Mercy

"Can you feel it? The world is emptying of meaning, the substance of relationships vanishing, the qualia of reality thinning."

My eyes widen as you say this. I know these symptoms.

"We need to get you to a metaphysiologist *now*," I tell you firmly.

"The connections will be too tenuous soon. Everything's going to be dissociated," you murmur, voice growing faint.

To you, everything is dissolving, dissipating into nebulous aether, losing all coherence. Which means your consciousness is rarefying, and there's no time to lose. I crouch down in front of you and grab behind me for your thighs. Serendipitously, your torso flops forward upon my back as I pull you away from the park bench and stand up. I struggle to shift you into a suitable position, and once you seem pretty steady, I start walking, leaving behind your bag of chips, planning out in my mind the fastest route to the mental health center.

No sooner have I taken a few steps than a few of the storefronts ahead of us along the street become fuzzy. Panic-stricken by this indication that your condition is spreading to me, I struggle to pick up the pace. Cars driving by take on a strange haziness, as if volatile and evaporating. The air feels intermittently stale and pasty. Some of the clouds in the sky turn translucent, then transparent. Trunks of trees disappear, leaving floating foliage. Then, portions of the scene around me become baffling or incomprehensible, estranged from any meaning in my mind; there's merely movement, color and sound with little construable cause and effect.

But swaths of my perception remain intact, allowing me to forge onward. The sidewalk beneath my feet stays stable, and the streets maintain their familiar shapes and arrangements.

Then, as the sky flickers between brilliance and darkness, a patch of it catches my attention. In the corner of my eye, I see a piece of sky that's unswervingly blue. I pause in my tracks and turn my head for a better look, startled to find that it's actually a sizable portion of sky that's normal and that beneath it, a community garden and the narrow roads around the garden look just as they should. In fact, everything behind us looks fine. I turn my entire body around, to more fully survey this tract of urban neighborhood we've been moving away from, but the moment I've reoriented us, everything that looked normal begins to deteriorate. The raised garden beds have become grainy and wobble like agitated gelatin. To compare this to what was ahead of us a moment ago, I turn my head back to the dissolving cityscape we've been heading toward. Now it's whole and utterly mundane, as if the trees, buildings and cars had coalesced while my back was turned to them, instantly re-forming themselves and accurately out of the chaos they were becoming.

Then a wave of urgency and panic about your condition sweeps through me, and I resume hurtling towards the mental health center. And seemingly just in time. I've traversed less than a block when everything ahead of us is very evidently breaking down again, like some confused, tumultuous melting and vaporizing of reality. I try to make sense of this while doing my dash-waddle down the street. Could there be something about looking back that stabilizes the world?

Then it dawns upon me that when I had my head turned, you were still facing straight ahead. Could it be then that I'm experiencing your perceptions combined with mine, and that when we're experiencing different parts of the world, I see my part of the world as I normally would? If that's true, then the things before us that are dissolving away should appear normal for me when you're not perceiving them. To test this, I slow to a stop and look at the mailbox just down the sidewalk from us. It's turning into a wavy hodgepodge of green and purple. I reorient us so it's behind us, then turn my head to look at it. But instead of seeing the mailbox as I normally would, I see nothing there. In fact, all the things that were losing form and meaning are gone. The mailbox, blurs of parked cars, cloudy street signs, garbled birdsongs, they've vanished.

I turn us back in the direction of the mental health center, and some of the parked cars reappear. My eyes widen at the implications. Could it be that your experiences are what give parts of the world their reality? Does this apply to all of us? That together we make the world real for ourselves and each other? Is that why parts of the world aren't fading into meaninglessness, because I or others perceive them? If so, then it should be no problem getting you to the mental health center. While you may be disbanding facets of the world, I'm also giving the world cohesiveness. Pondering this, I hasten towards the mental health facility, hoping the specialists there can give me a more definitive sense of what's going on here.

As we near the center, my back and arms start to feel numb. Carrying you all this way must be taking its toll. You're much heavier than any backpack I've ever carried. Despite the loss of feeling, I'm sure I can make it the rest of the way. But then as I glance at my arms, I notice they're lacking definite shape, definite boundaries with you and the air about us.

I search for somewhere to set you down. I head into a small playground, what's left of it, and manage to seat you upon one of the swings. Slumped forward into a flaccid heap, you're utterly dazed. Then I turn my attention to myself and find that I can only feel my hands as a vague tingle, that they look as if made out of vapor. If your conscious experience is affecting the world, it's affecting me now. That could mean there are no limits to how far the degeneration of the world could spread. The erosion of your consciousness may lead to that of my own and others.

I have to go get help. There's no way I can carry you any further as I—my existence unravels.

But then it occurs to me that if this is what's really going on, that your mind shapes reality including me, then I should be able to reshape you. How am I supposed to do that? I struggle to reason this out, because though it may not be applicable, besides panic, reason is all I've got at my disposal now. Mustering what concentration I can, I get my thoughts to coalesce into tentative conclusions.

If we're all engaged in the cobbling together of reality without our knowing it, the process must be largely unconscious. There are only scant avenues I have for communicating with my unconscious mind, the most promising of which seems to be autosuggestion.

Sitting down in the swing beside you, I close my eyes and tell myself that the world is whole, and that your consciousness is unified in lucid perception of world and self. I envision you and our surroundings as I've known them, my attention focused steadily upon these thoughts to fill and inculcate my mind with them. Then, deep in a mental era of singular, basic understanding, I feel time become languid, all my perceptions aligning with my fundamental experience of you.

And after the passage of subjective eons, I'm ready to open my eyes and face our reality.

When Grooming is Just Caressing

All morning, I've been eagerly awaiting your—our—afternoon appointment. As I cleaned and then massaged the minds of today's first batch of clientele, I became increasingly impatient to stroke your thoughts. You take such good care of your psychological constitution, you have almost none of the debris, parasites and junk that take up residence in the knotted conceptions and feelings of the other minds I groom. I don't have to pick out little errors in reasoning, use harsh abrasives to scrub down the callousness of excessive self-importance, wear gloves to handle the jagged or caustic misconceptions, rebuff lackluster pride…. Cleansing your mind is really just a refreshing rinse, for both of us.

Unlike my nine-thirty. *Ugh.* What a way to start the day. The guy should really book a full hour for all the mental maintenance he needs, but he never does, so every week I have only half an hour to do something along the lines of what I did this morning:

- scrape away fragments of unneeded, self-deprecating memory on the verge of being forgotten yet clinging obstinately to the self-narrative;
- clip off petty annoyances, those shards of thought that have splintered off from expectations and can lead to irritability;
- pry from the nooks and crannies of his subconscious the trivial expectations of acquaintances, colleagues, friends— society—each almost innocuous but collectively applying troubling, omnidirectional pressure upon his identity;
- rub the copious amounts of salve upon his conscience

that he wouldn't need if his metaphysiology weren't so off balance.

And somehow I managed to get all this done and clear up his mind pretty nicely. A substantial, even impressive accomplishment, but with regulars like him, I can feel only incredibly fleeting satisfaction because you know it's going to be a mess again by the next week. If he didn't have his appointments the same weekday as yours, I don't think I'd be as patient with him. Sure, that admission is pretty unprofessional, but while we're skilled specialists, we're only human—there's only so much we can tolerate.

Now, as I eat a tofu banh mi for lunch in the building's little courtyard, I wonder why you even come here. Maybe you like to be thorough in the maintenance of your mental health, wanting another caretaker to verify your efforts, to check on the parts difficult for you to reach. But honestly, it almost feels like sometimes I should be paying you because working on your thoughts is a sheer delight. When I'm massaging your supple mind, it often feels like I'm simply and happily fondling your imagination, caressing your emotions, tickling your curiosity. I hope that you enjoy it as much as (or, if at all possible, more than) I do. I want to treat your thoughts and emotions the way the warm sunlight touches my cheek right now—insubstantially but unmistakably transmitting a vital energy.

The moment I come back into the salon, my nostrils fill with the chemical odor of the psychoactives applied generously to preempt the growth of everything from neurotic worries to obsessive tendencies, that familiar olfactory bouquet of pharmacological achievements, none of which will be used on you. As I head to prep a room for my next client, I have to actively suppress the grin that threatens to burst hugely upon my face because there are just two appointments to go until yours.

"Hey," Risa calls out to me from the booking desk. "Your two-thirty can't make it."

Stopping in my tracks, my heart sinks as my energy disperses into the air. That's your time slot.

"I've moved that session to six-thirty, assuming you can stay late," Risa adds.

"Yeah, yeah, that's no problem," I quickly say, my energy rapidly coalescing back into me.

My heart leaps as if trying to somersault within my chest.

"Great," Risa replies, nodding. "Should be worth it. You'll probably get a nice fat tip for the schedule change and after-hours work."

"Yeah, maybe, but I don't mind going the extra mile for our lovely regulars," I remark. "They deserve it."

"True," she agrees, grinning.

A fat tip, sure, that would be nice. But Risa and I both know the upshot here is already going to be more than enough; wrapping up my day and starting my evening with your voluptuous mind, that will be a treat, especially if you've got no pressing evening plans to rush off to. And honestly, I don't know if I could stand to wait another week to get my hands on your mind.

The Consequences of Self Storage

Mere minutes into my evening shift at the self storage center, there you are, standing with arms crossed, eyes sharp, on the other side of the reception desk.

"Hi," you say with a hint of urgency before I can greet you with the pleasantries I've been trained to conduct.

"Hi. Is there something I can help you with?" I ask, putting down my croissant.

"I can't get my locker open," you quickly answer.

"Let's go have a look," I reply.

I pull open the bottom right drawer of the front desk and take out the small toolkit that's kept there. No sooner have I scooted my chair out from the desk than you're heading into the facility. Toting the toolkit by its kid-lunchbox-style handle, I follow after you, down the narrow, metallic corridors lined with locked doors of varying sizes.

You sail through the inert air full of fluorescent lighting, the vibrance of your clothes a severe contrast with our thoroughly gray, faintly nutmeg facility environs. You are a collection of rhythmically rearranging blue stripes, beige flutters, iron-creased angles and gleaming metal, a fluid fragment of the outside world breezing through here as dynamic and ephemeral chromaticity. The way you quickly—effortlessly—navigate the maze of storage units without the slightest pause for consideration or orientation, you must be a regular here. I've seen you come in several times since starting this job, but surely you also come here when I'm not on duty.

Soon we're at the cluster of small lockers, the ones that are just a little larger than safe deposit boxes.

"This one," you tell me, pointing to one in the corner about a meter from the floor.

"Okay, I'll try the master key. Sometimes that works."

"There's *a master key*? I thought I had the only key."

"You have the only unique key," I tell you. "The only one that specifically fits this lock. There's a master key that fits all the locks in the facility, for security purposes. It's mentioned in the terms of your storage agreement, but hardly anyone reads the whole thing."

"*Security purposes*? The fact that you can open all of these with a single key makes me feel that it's *less secure*."

"I assure you, we take the proper precautions with the master key. We keep it accounted for at all times, and it has anti-duplication technology embedded in it," I explain. "It's worth the slight risk that someone might misuse it. This key allows us to access items that might be problematic. Say some stale emotions were turning noxious. We would need to be able to get to those feelings and quarantine them properly. Or if you lost your key, we'd use the master key to get your stuff out."

"Well, all right. I can understand how a master key could be necessary."

"Yes. It could cost precious time if we had to search for a specific duplicate key during an emergency. And if we somehow took the wrong key to a locker causing concern deep in the facility, it all might end disastrously. Also, this way, you have the only unique key, as you know."

"That makes sense," you say hurriedly.

I take the rapidity of your words as a cue to get on with it and use the master key, which I was about to do anyways. I insert the key and turn it clockwise, finding surprising resistance. I jiggle the key as I apply more force to keep turning it, but I can only get it to go about half the rotation needed to open the locker. So I remove the key and take a small oil applicator from the toolbox. The applicator's beak deposits a few drops of oil just inside the keyhole. I then use a thin furry brush to spread the oil around the internal workings of the lock.

"Try your key now," I tell you.

You insert it and get it to turn about three-quarters of the way, but then the lock remains stubbornly stuck. After you've removed your key, I try the master key again, only to get about the same results.

"Sorry, but I'll have to get someone from the maintenance crew to work on this," I conclude.

I've reached the limits of what I can do here. I haven't been trained to do anything more involved than the use of the master key and lubricant.

"*Aw man*," you grouse. "Is there nothing else that can be done? Can you at least give me another locker temporarily or something?"

"Of course. We have a secure vault for short-term storage."

"All right," you reply impatiently.

You check your watch, then ask, "Can you put my… personal belongings in there? I'm pressed for time."

"Certainly," I reply. "Once your locker is repaired, your belongings will be transferred to it from the vault."

"Great."

Without another word, you hand me a warm, pulsating, cloth-wrapped bundle. The soft heat is immediately familiar, but the firm vividness of its temperature is new and surprising to me.

"No problem, and sorry for the inconvenience," I answer.

"Have a nice date," I can't stop myself from adding.

Your eyes dart to meet mine, intense with surprise. Slowly you smile, and then you head off briskly, leaving me standing by your locker.

Then, moving down the corridors at a leisurely, almost sluggish pace, I hold your swaddled heart in one hand, the toolkit in the other. I'm looking forward to getting back to my croissant.

But when I arrive at the front desk, a man is there waiting for me.

"I need to get some hope I stashed here," he tells me. "I just remembered it expires later this week and came here straight from work, so I don't have my key."

"Okay, I'll need your storage unit designation and government-issued ID," I tell him.

"Yeah, r3-62w," he says.

I type those alphanumerics into the computer and pull up his profile.

"And here's my driver's license," he says, holding it out to me.

He looks just like the picture we have on file, but I check the name and address on his license as I've been instructed to.

"All right, just give me a moment," I tell him.

I won't be able to put your heart in the vault until after I take care of this. So once I've taken the master key from the toolkit, I place both the toolkit and your heart in the bottom right drawer, then lock the drawer with the key kept in the middle drawer, which I then pocket.

"Let's go," I then say to him.

We trek our way deep into the convolutions of basement 2, into an area I recognize as where people embarking upon diets leave their appetites. r3-62w is among the walk-in units here, and this time there's no difficulty with the lock. The storage unit opens right up. Then I have to avert my eyes. Not because the contents might be highly personal (they very well might be), but because the interior is luxuriantly luminous to the point of being visually painful.

Prepared for this, the man dons sunglasses and flaps open a sailcloth bag, then strides right in. While he's in there, presumably gathering up the hope on the verge of expiring, I look down the hallway, my gaze held away from the uncomfortable brightness. A few minutes later, he's out, closing the door behind him, the now bulging, glowing bag clutched in his other hand.

"Thanks," he says, holding up the bag to indicate that he's all set.

"Great," I reply, then lock up the unit.

We begin backtracking, the route we took just minutes ago feeling familiar as we run it in reverse.

As we're ascending a flight of stairs, I catch a whiff of smoke. At first I think maybe this guy had a cigarette before coming in, but then I notice faint, hazy tendrils rising from the bag. My eyes widen at this.

"Is that hope burning up?" I ask him.

"No, it's still good until at least tomorrow," he assures me.

But a moment later, he recoils from the bag. It drops to the floor, contents blasting white hot light all over the place, wispy tendrils of dark smoke writhing upward.

"I'll get a fire extinguisher," I tell him.

I rush to the closest door and enter a subcorridor of basement 1. My eyes race frantically around the walls for a fire extinguisher. Seeing none, I head down the hallway. A right and two lefts later, to my partial relief, I find one. I grab it out of its niche in the wall and dash back the way I came. Except it turns out not to be the way I came, because I don't end up back at the stairwell entrance. But a few minutes later, I do, and I get back to where the guy is.

There's no blazing light now.

"Sorry about that," he says. "Agitating it must've turned the stuff reactive. I tempered it down with the cool reason I keep on hand."

"Okay, glad that's all taken care of," I manage to say while catching my breath.

"Yeah, sorry. I had forgotten how sensitive this stuff can be."

I nod.

"Well, I've got to put this thing back. You can just head out from here," I tell him, breaking protocol. I should escort him, but he doesn't seem the snooping type, and I can check the security cameras later to make sure he's out.

"You know the way, right?" I ask.

"I think so. If not, I'll call you over the intercom system."

"All right, I'll go take care of this then," I reply, slapping a hand on the fire extinguisher's metal body.

When I at last get back to the front desk, I unlock the bottom drawer to put the master key back into the toolkit and to move your belongings to the vault. When I pull the drawer open, I jump back because your heart is jumping. Or not jumping exactly, but lightly bouncing in its cloth wrapping upon the top of the toolkit. I wasn't expecting this, and startled by it, I feel as though my own heart is bouncing around in my chest. I take its vigorous activity as a sign that your date must be off to a good start.

I consider resting my hand on your heart to feel it hammering mightily. The sensation of that upon my palm and fingertips is bound to be stunning—euphoric no doubt.

But handling your heart that way would be unprofessional. And I will get to feel some of its gleeful oscillations as I take it to the vault.

I wonder if you regret leaving it here.

Ménage à Trois

I

"I need your help while I'm away," your boyfriend says as we're wrapping up our session in the ceramics studio.

I hang up my clay-smeared smock and reply, "Okay," thinking this is going to be about some errand or loose end he hasn't been able to take care of.

"So you know how we haven't... well, of course, there's never been any reason until now for us to," he begins, and I know he's not talking about him and me in the ceramics studio, the pronouns we and us used once again in that subtly emphatic way that can only refer to you and him as a couple.

"You know, we've never gone... LDR," he says, at last getting to the point, speaking this acronym as if the initials of a notorious villain—one who has undone the harmony and aspirations of so many couples.

Long Distance Relationship.

This is going to be more serious than I expected.

"So I'm going to give her all my love before I leave," he tells me.

Skeptical, I ask, "Are you sure it's wise to take a one-shot approach?"

I lean against the counter beside me.

"You know I'm all about front-loading my endeavors. And this is where you come in. If this stash of love I'm giving her starts running low, I need you to replenish it."

"How? Are you leaving a second... stash with me?"

"No, like I said, I'm giving her *all* my love, and I mean that. I'm asking you to… contribute your love."

I imagine myself going into your room while you're out or taking a shower, finding the diminishing cache of love and augmenting it with my own love. It strikes me as utterly crazy—underhanded, to say the least.

"Are you sure about this?" I ask.

"Yeah," is all you say.

"But won't she know? I mean, if the love is dwindling, she's going to notice that there's suddenly more or that it's not running out."

"Right, so I'm going to tell her that I'll be shipping her my newfound and freshly cultivated love for her while I'm away by sending them in packages to you."

"But why would you ship it to me?"

"Because you can receive deliveries at work, and she's got classes and things during the day. And if you were sending someone your love, you wouldn't want it just sitting out on the apartment building steps or even in the hallway, right?"

"Yeah, I guess I'd send it by certified mail," I consider, then think aloud, "So you want me to give her my love in… empty packages you send, so it looks like it's coming from abroad?"

"Basically."

"Why not send her more love for real?"

"Because I'm giving her *all* my love. It's going to take a while to recoup that kind of down payment. And when there's more to give, of course, I'll give that to her, but in the meantime…"

He prods my arm with his elbow.

"You're sure?"

"Definitely," he says with confidence that feels inappropriate, unwarranted—excessively entrepreneurial.

Still dubious, I rephrase my skepticism as, "I don't know if this will work."

"But you're pretty generous with your love because it's not tied up in a relationship. Unless there's something that's come up. Is there a special someone that—"

"No, it's not that. I mean, it'll be a disaster if we're caught."

"Why would we get caught? She trusts me, she trusts you."

"Yeah, and we're going to be abusing that trust."

"Well, I don't agree with how you're framing it, but whatever it is we'd be doing, it's because I—we care about her. You care about her, you care about me, right? So just think of it as like the love you'd give me, you'd be giving that to her, for me. And it may not even come to this. I'm giving her plenty of love before I go."

"Yeah, but it's still sneaky, and something could go wrong."

"Like I said, this is just a contingency plan. So we can figure out the details when—if it goes into action."

I think about this for a moment. It would be better to have a backup plan that isn't deceptive and dishonest, but I know LDRs can be hard and having this outlandish fallback scenario will help put his mind at ease.

"Okay, so how will I know the plan is going live?" I ask.

He smiles and says, "I'll give you the go-ahead. But you have to look for signs that it needs to go into effect."

"You want me to check on... the stash?"

"If you can, but also pay attention to her behavior, prod with the occasional question or comment. You already have a pretty good idea of when she needs attention and when she's feeling down. If you start to sense something, call me immediately."

"All right. I can do that."

"Good," he says, smiling.

That seems to conclude matters, and we finish tidying up.

2

For a while, everything is just fine. You're chipper as can be. It's like you're just not going to see him for a week, like you're only separated by the span of several days rather than indefinite months. Our domestic life carries on largely as it always has.

Then gradually, your mood begins to darken. You talk less energetically, spend significantly more time than usual on school work—seemingly because it's the meaningful, preoccupying enterprise you need to dedicate your effort to anyways, not because there's more of it. You spend more and more time on the university campus, in its cafés and libraries, working, thinking, not talking and not dreaming. I become concerned but don't want to react prematurely. Maybe this just needs to run its course, and you'll find for yourself the solutions you need.

Two and a half weeks into the LDR, you tell me you'll be coming home late because of a class project. I'm finishing my breakfast before work and surprised by your announcement.

"Should I leave some dinner out for you?" I ask, losing all interest in the remaining corner of toast I'm holding.

"No, by late, I mean really late. I'll eat out," you answer plainly.

I just answer, "Okay," and eat the uninteresting bit of toast to offer the semblance of normalcy to you.

After swallowing this mundane mouthful of barely buttered bread, I decide that since your condition hasn't improved any, I must seize the opportunity afforded by your absence.

Throughout the hours that follow at work, I sporadically fantasize about stealthily scouring your room. Fortunately, this doesn't get me into any trouble, but my creative partner notices my distraction and asks if something is on my mind. Too lazy to be dishonest or more honest, I tell her that there is but that it's not a big deal.

In the evening, I go into your room and search all over for

the love you were given, dreading that my suspicions will be confirmed. I see bits of love everywhere: in the closet, desk drawers, coat pockets, on the dresser, your pillows, shelves and nightstand. But all that's not nearly as much love as I expected to find. Then at last, I uncover the remainder of the "stash" under your bed. And there can be no mistake; it's getting precariously low. I have no idea what the original amount was, but in its current state, it can't last much longer. And it's getting stale.

I start to wonder if you're out not working but socializing—prospecting or engaging other sources of love.

I shake my head frantically. I know you better than that. You wouldn't handle things that way. And even if you really felt like you wanted to do that, you'd talk to me first, right? Or maybe not since there's some chance I might tell your boyfriend even if you told me not to, but I feel like I would have at least seen some signs if you were seeking out love from others.

And why is there so little love left? Maybe you've overindulged yourself, the abundance of love seeming initially inexhaustible, overriding your better judgment to preserve it. Or maybe you've become needier, or you've always been needy and I've never really known.

Then I realize that aside from the occasional letter and infrequent phone call, there is only the love he has given you. That is the only presence he has here beyond your memories and some photographs. If I were in such a situation, I would undoubtedly come to rely on a "stash" of love more and more.

Ignoring the time difference between us and the expense, I rush to my room, grab for the phone, and call him.

"*Already?*" he blurts once I've hurriedly explained the situation.

"Yeah, I can barely believe it myself."

"Okay, this is exactly what we've discussed. You know where

we're heading with this, right?"

"Yes," I answer, stunned by how easily I said that.

"Good. So I'm going to send a box later this afternoon. You should get it in a couple days."

"All right, make it a fairly sizable box."

"Got it. I've got to get back to work, but call me if anything happens."

"Okay. Goodbye."

"Bye."

Nervously I wait for you to come home, trying to read a novel on the couch. After several restlessly read chapters, you at last return—after midnight!

When you come inside and see the lights still on, you call out, "Oh, you're still up?"

"Yeah. I didn't really feel like sleeping," I tell you.

"Are you okay?" you ask, voice heavy with fatigue but still carrying your concern to me.

"Yeah," I say, probably unconvincingly, so I add, "Did the project work go well?"

"I think we have the bulk of the groundwork done."

"Can I see?" I blurt out.

"Well, okay, if you really want to. It's still really rough," you tell me, opening your portfolio case.

You array a series of pages on the kitchen table.

"So here's the general outline, and there's the flow we intend to follow," you tell me, pointing to components of the case study strategy before us, like you're showing me features of a wide landscape through a set of narrow windows.

Looking at all the sketched out storyboards and diagrams, I heave a huge sigh of relief.

"Are you really all right?" you ask.

"Yeah, I am now."

"What do you mean?"

"It's just that... I know how much this project means to you and all," I quickly say.

"Oh... that's sweet of you," you say, placing a hand on my shoulder, and I feel absolutely awful for lying to you and for suspecting—no matter how briefly—that you were out doing something else.

But there's no turning back, and I reply, "Well, I know how hard you've been working on it, and I really hope it goes well for you."

"Is that what kept you up?"

"No, I was thinking about something."

"I see. If you want to, we could talk about it, after I take a shower or tomorrow."

"It's just... work. I don't want to trouble you with that. I know you have a lot going on."

"Are you sure? I don't mind."

"Yeah, it might just work itself out."

"Nice pun," you remark, smiling faintly.

"What was?" I ask, puzzled.

"That whatever work you're worried about might *work* itself out."

"Oh, how observant of you, for this time of night."

"Yeah, I surprise myself too. All right then," you say, withdrawing your hand. "In that case, I'm going to get ready for bed."

3

Three days later, I get the box, which is half the size of a carton of milk. He's sealed it very sparsely and loosely with tape, so it'll be easy to open and reseal. Inside, there is only a short note.

This is the largest size box I could send you quickly and economically. I'll send more semi-regularly.

With a petulance that surprises me, I tear up the note and put the scraps into the recycling bin.

I wrap up everything I have to do for the day as quickly as I can and leave the office early. I head home, nervous, afraid that this isn't going to work, that you're going to see right through the ruse. My heart is erratically jumpy during the entire train ride back, lurching every time I make incidental eye contact with someone.

As I had hoped, I get home before you do and shut myself in my room. With the open box placed on my desk, I take a deep breath and start filling the interior with my love, careful not to pack it too densely. Once I'm satisfied with the composition and arrangement of the contents, I tape up the box. Then I try to distract myself from this crazy scheme by doing the laundry. I don't even have a full load of clothing to wash, but I need an activity to busy myself with. So I take what I've got down to the laundry room in our apartment building's basement.

Once my clothes are in the washing machine and I'm back in our apartment, I get to work cleaning up my room, starting with the stacks of miscellaneous books that have accumulated beside my desk.

When you get home, I'm in the middle of cooking dinner.

"I got a package for you," I tell you.

I leave the pan-frying zucchini unattended for a moment and pick up the box on the counter.

"And I think I know what's in here!" I try to say playfully as I hold it out towards you.

Grinning almost deliriously, you eagerly take the box, practically snatching it out of my hands.

"Thanks!" you shout, prancing off to your room.

You don't emerge from your room until dinner is ready. As we eat, you're quiet, in a dreamy mood—undoubtedly euphoric with the delights of this (from your perspective) new, fresh love of his. You seem utterly lost in your thoughts and emotions, eating while barely aware that you're eating.

In the evening, while we're lounging in our little living room, listening to ambient trance, you remark, "His love is pretty different now—feels more serious… simple and sincere."

"Oh, well, you know, people change, especially when they're in a different place," I reply as nonchalantly as I can, still looking at the magazine I'm holding.

"Yeah, that's true. Funny though, it's more like your love."

My eyes lift from the colorful page to meet your eyes.

"That is pretty funny," I reply, chasing my words with a hearty bout of feigned laughter. "Who would've ever thought he'd become more like me that way!"

"Yeah, what're the odds," you say, smiling enigmatically— somewhat unnervingly.

I sense you are insinuating that I have something to do with this, so I try to turn the tables by saying, "But what do you know about my love anyways?"

"Oh, I've caught glimpses of it now and then, heard about it from friends and of course *received* some from you."

"But only a little, as friends," I say hastily.

"Oh, you'd be surprised how much you can learn from a little bit of love."

"I see. Well, I'm flattered that you think his love is akin to my own."

You raise an eyebrow and ask, "Should you be?"

"Well, not that I'm conceited or anything, but I do feel like my love is of reasonably good quality."

You nod thoughtfully, your silence making me uneasy.

I try to regain my wits by shifting the subject to something more comfortable but still related to the conversation at hand.

"Any letter in the package?" I ask. "There might be clues to why his love has changed."

"No, no letter. But I did get one recently, just a couple days ago. It didn't mention anything that suggests why his love is changing."

I'm afraid I'm digging myself deeper into this hole.

"Maybe he doesn't know yet that he's changing. Maybe he's changing in ways he hasn't noticed."

"Yeah, that's certainly possible," you say, nodding.

"I think I've been changing, and I'm just starting to notice," you add after a moment. "I wonder when that started happening."

"It's tough being apart?"

"Sometimes."

4

In the following days, I get another box.

Fearing that you're on to me, I mix into my love some jealousy and insecurity. I figure this will be fairly convincing. He could be envious of people around here, because they get to see you in person and spend more time with you. And maybe as he's meeting new people and encountering new ideas; he could be feeling uncertain about his dynamic with you, wondering if he should give you more attention or be more sensitive.

Introducing these emotions into my love turns out to be easier than I thought. Oddly enough, at heart temperature, the jealousy just blends right into the raw love with just a little stirring. I pack up about half of this new formulation of love, setting the rest aside for later "shipments"—the next several boxes, over which I'll slowly increase the ratio of envy and doubt.

After a long day in the office, I give you the second box. Despite being worn out, I anxiously await your reaction. But to my surprise, during the rest of the evening and the days following, you make no mention of his love, allaying my fears. You appear to be simply content, even hopeful. This allows me to become less preoccupied by my third-wheel status in your romantic life, that feeling that I'm the one training wheel left on a bicycle that shouldn't need it—hoping that I'm not part of a tricycle.

Then, by all indications, life reverts to the early days of your LDR. Apparently refreshed and renewed by the love, you're more spirited, more colorful in our dinnertime and evening conversations. When your schoolwork allows, we do more of our once customary activities: jamming with you on drums and me on vibraphone, pole vaulting, indulging in impromptu karaoke sessions and binging on acclaimed art house films.

This renaissance of personal activity takes place as your class projects have only become more demanding. Impressively you're making substantial time for physical and social activity by working more effectively. You're extremely focused when it comes to schoolwork, regularly quarantining yourself away from me by closing the door to your room, from others by going to the little-known recesses of the library. You rigorously draft and hold yourself to to-do lists. Then when you've completed the day's tasks, work is pushed from the forefront of your mind to the back, muzzled or given chew toys so it cannot gnaw at even the edges of your consciousness.

You'd only have the energy to do this if your spirits have been lifted. Love has a knack for doing just this kind of elevating.

Very quickly, I settle into our new dynamic, embracing this new energy, marveling that his plan is actually working.

5

"It's changed again," you tell me a couple weeks later.

We're sitting on the sofa, turned lethargic by a hearty dinner.

"Oh, well, you know love is like that. People are like that," I say casually.

"Yeah, but it's making me worry this time. It makes me feel like he's becoming more unsure—not unsure of me but how he's treating me."

"Well, it can't be rosy all the time. Everyone has uncertainties, and distance can really amplify them."

"I'm... concerned that his feelings might start wavering," you say quietly. "Maybe they already have."

"Why don't you send him some love? I'm sure he'd really appreciate that."

"Oh... well, I'm not so sure about that," you say quietly, surprising me. "You see, I've started to have my own doubts about this relationship—not about him but about the situation, our circumstances. About myself too. I don't know if I can keep doing this, if this is going to work."

I become apprehensive that I've made matters worse by trying to make the ploy more authentic. I take a deep breath to keep myself from panicking.

"I guess you should give it some more time," I say slowly. "There are bound to be ups and downs. And talking or writing about it might help. I'm sure he'd appreciate your honest thoughts about... the situation."

"You're probably right. I just feel like I need to sort some of this out first."

"Well, I'll help you do that, if you want. And maybe talking things through with him will help you do that too. It could also help him with his... concerns."

You give this a moment of consideration, then answer, "Okay, maybe we can talk about it tomorrow or the day after. I think I need to take some time to get my thoughts together."

"I understand. We can talk whenever you want to."

"Thanks," you say quietly and reach over to place your hand on mine.

Then you rise from the sofa and head to your room. I listen to its door slowly creak before shutting with a click.

6

"*What happened?*" he almost shouts the moment I pick up the phone, and I'm almost sure what he wants to ask—demand is, "What did you do?"

Despite the urgency, I manage to explain everything chronologically and coherently.

"So we talked through her feelings and thoughts—but I didn't say anything that I thought would be biased. I tried to listen carefully and be supportive. And she decided that she probably needs a break to better understand herself and this relationship," I tell him, wrapping up my recount.

"Well, did you try to be supportive of my side of things?" he asks immediately.

"To the extent that I could, I most definitely did."

"I mean, I did give her all of my love, and I think that really says a lot."

"I'm sure it did. But there's much more involved beyond quantities of love."

He sighs heavily.

"Okay," he says, beginning a new chapter of our conversation in a quieter voice. "I know you didn't mean to precipitate a dramatic turn of events, to upset a balance that we didn't know was so precarious."

I nod, even though he of course can't see. The motion makes me feel better, especially since it distracts me even if only slightly from waiting for what he'll say next.

After the brief pause, he continues, "All right, I'm going to send her all the love I have for her as soon as I can."

"I suppose that could help," I reply.

There is a certain appealing plausibility in what he proposes. If you at last receive his love and feel its intensity and resolve, you'll be assured of the strength of this relationship and of your own feelings. It's worth a shot. I don't have a better—or really any alternative.

"I think you should use the fastest shipping method available," I add.

7

In the office mailroom, I find a box adorned in foreign postage and shipping labels, addressed in his handwriting, hurriedly with fat-tipped marker. A couple of the box's corners are dented, and the top is deformed, sagging considerably inwards like something heavy has been placed on it at some point. Overcome with concern, I start to carefully open it right there. As I begin handling the box, I notice that it feels strangely light.

Slowly and anxiously, I loosen the tape sealing it so that I can reseal it without making you suspicious. Fortunately, the cardboard constituting the box has been laminated with some kind of glossy coating (probably to make it water-resistant enough to endure some light rain or heavy fog) and this makes it fairly easy to remove the tape without making the box look like it's obviously been tampered with.

Several nerve-wracking minutes later, I've got the tape off, and I'm unfolding the cardboard flaps.

"Urgent delivery?" a coworker asks, startling me. I didn't even notice him walk in.

"Uh, yeah," I reply distractedly.

"I don't think I've ever seen anyone open a package right here, on the spot," he remarks.

"Yeah, well, you know, this time-sensitive material," I murmur, not sure what I'm even trying to say.

But apparently it doesn't matter. He nods and smiles a bit, then walks out with the envelopes he's just collected.

I return my full attention to the box. Removing the tissue paper padding the contents, I glimpse the radiance of his love for you through gaps in the furoshiki it's enfolded within, but the love looks like it's in fragments, pieces much smaller than I'd expect.

Fearing that it's been damaged in transit—maybe by the pressure of heavy items placed upon it or rough handling—I hurriedly unwrap the cloth-bound love, feeling its warmth. I look at the luminous pieces of love wondering if they can be put back together if they're warmed up or joined by some raw love. But then I realize they were never part of one coherent whole; their shapes and emotional contents aren't complementary, meaning they were disparate pieces of love to start with—nothing like what I saw of the diminishing stash of love under your bed. How is that possible? If that love was so cohesive, how could this love be such a jumble?

Amid my confusion, I realize that someone else could walk in at any moment, and it would look very unprofessional to be preoccupied by a package of love during work hours. I fold the furoshiki over the love and put the tissue paper back in the box.

Walking with languid, heavy steps, I carry the box back to my team's work area. On my way, I get the feeling that this is love he's scraped together, still fledgling and rather amorphous.

Maybe he is still romantically set back from giving you all of his love; after all, he did expect to have more time to nurture new feelings from emotional scratch. Or perhaps he hasn't had the time to cultivate his love for you with the kind of dedication necessary, or the environment there isn't conducive to its maturation.

I know what I have to do. But this will be the last time I'm going to be this mixed up in your relationship with him.

I place the box on my desk.

"I'm not feeling well," I tell my partner, walking over to her desk. "I think I should go home and get some rest."

"Oh, okay. Yeah, you don't look so good," she replies. "I hope you're not coming down with something," she adds, pressing her hand to my forehead. "You actually are kind of hot."

It's the anxiety. It's making me flushed.

"Hopefully I'll feel better once I can rest a little," I tell her.

"All right. Just call me if you aren't coming in tomorrow," she says.

8

At my desk, with the door to my room closed, I hold the bits of love just close enough to my heart to soften them up. With all the concentration I can muster, I take the ones that most closely resemble each other and fit them together, joining them when necessary with my own love or complementary emotions like trust and wistfulness.

After what feels like hours of this, I lean back in my desk chair, exhausted. I've done all that I can with what he's given you. From here, it's up to you and him.

As the Past Tries to Catch Up
With You: Part 7

With the arrival of winter's chill, you're becoming overtly antsy. I can tell you're eager to just pick a direction and go, even if it's ultimately counterproductive. Because the longer you're here, the more hopeless and restless you feel.

"The trail's gone so cold it could freeze methane," you lament this morning while lingering in the kitchen after our breakfast of natto on toast.

You're slumped in what's now your usual seat at the kitchen table, and I'm leaning against the refrigerator door, each of us not quite ready to head out to our respective workplaces.

"Why don't we both take the day off," I suggest. "We can go somewhere so you can digest the situation or get it off your mind, whichever you need to do. I don't have any pressing tasks for the rest of this week. And I could use a break from the serious atmosphere of the lab."

"I don't have anything pressing either," you answer. "As long as my current project gets done before the end-of-the-month deadline, I'll be fine."

"So how about we go to the auditory obstacle course? I could use a listening workout, and then afterwards we can take it easy in the harbor area."

"Great idea."

My mind feels comfortably flaccid as we sit wordlessly together on one of the piers extending into the foggy waters, exhausted but exhilarated.

"What a deep, vibrant soundscape with challenging noises," I say at last.

"Definitely," you agree, zipping your jacket all the way up. "Exploring and navigating it was strenuous and tremendously satisfying in the end. I'm really glad we came. Thanks for getting us out of our routines."

"No problem."

You have that fatigued but contented air about you, slouching forward, eyes seemingly fixed upon a world woven into the interstices of ours. Looking at you here reminds me of when we first met. That moment was like the first time I tasted root beer and found it delightfully new with hints of the familiar, a fresh synthesis of sweet, cool and effervescent sensations. Something about the experience made intuitive sense despite its novelty.

"I feel better," you remark. "But soon thoughts about him will be at the forefront of my mind again, trying to coalesce into a plan for tracking him down."

I'm hesitant to continue on this subject, but since you've brought it up, I ask, "Have you ever thought that the best thing a future self can do for you and other past selves is to work on what that future self feels is important?"

"Sometimes. But I think what's important to future selves of mine should have a strong connection to what's important to me. At least some of it. I feel so strongly about my perspectives and goals that I can't bear to let them go forsaken by a future self. I really want him to continue developing the ideas I formulated. I need him to so I can see what they can become and ultimately culminate in."

"I'm sure he knows that. And I'm also sure that even though he's trying to escape from you, he carries some of the same feelings you do, though maybe they've taken radically different forms. And a later future self may rediscover how important it is to strive towards what you hold so dear."

"I want to find your words reassuring, but knowing how much we've changed from self to self, I can't easily accept that perspective."

"Is fighting that change really going to be beneficial?" I ask, more pointedly than I had intended.

"The fact that I can't find him means that he places a very high value on the differences between us... He's clearly willing to devote tremendous energy to maintain those differences, and the energy we put into this hide-and-seek game could be better spent."

"Maybe you need to believe in the strength of your feelings. If they are really that intense and important, he's got to know how much they mean to you, and they must mean something to him. Maybe you need to have a little more trust in your selves and your feelings."

I almost regret this the moment after I've said it, afraid that these words are confrontational and hurtful. But one-and-a-half guessing this is as far as I get because I do believe in the words I've just said.

"Is that why you don't have past selves chasing you?" you ask. "They trust you with their future?"

"For the most part. I still hear their voices in my mind, often reminding me of what they—and I—believe are important, and I do feel guilty about not upholding some of their aspirations. But we have a level of trust that enables us to be comfortable with each other's autonomy. I probably won't go chasing after a future self of mine to achieve my aspirations because I trust her to be who she and I need her to be."

"I envy you. I don't know if I could have that kind of peace of mind with my future selves."

"Well, you could try and see what happens."
You nod thoughtfully.

Before we head back, we have to have the springbean salad this area is known for. So we stop by the café I go to just for that dish. We share a bowl of this savory salad while sitting at an outdoor table that looks out upon the harbor.

After we've eaten about half of it in a pensive silence, I am compelled to bring up the topic of future selves again.

"Are you afraid that the progress you've made on your ideas will be in vain if he or a later future self doesn't keep working on them?" I venture, at the risk of putting into interrogative form what's obvious to you, at the risk of also compromising the experience of the refreshing vegetables we're munching.

"Yes, and no," you reply, lowering your fork upon a napkin on the tabletop. "I've gotten these ideas into a form that's somewhat complete. But I think he can and should take them further, especially with the personal perspectives I strove to put together. I don't like to put it in these terms, but after all that I've done for him, I think I deserve a little more appreciation and respect. I don't want to go so far as to say that he owes me or is otherwise beholden to me, but I really put tremendous effort into creating mental clarity and positioning him intellectually, socially and financially. Which I admit he has built upon—even significantly in some ways—but he's left a good deal of potential unfulfilled."

The way you say this, I start to see him not as my friend and a skilled designer of eccentric impossibility spaces, but instead as your prodigal protégé or errant apprentice. I'm led from there to consider the opportunities afforded to me by my past selves that I've blown, and these thoughts cast faint shadows of doubt upon beliefs about my selves.

Have my past selves been too lenient on me or have we never felt as intensely about our ideas and ambitions as you do? Does the closeness among my selves come at the price of the permissiveness you accused me of? My mind tinges with despondency, but quiet, dearly held voices urge me to later take stock of my emotions before drawing even tentative conclusions. My thoughts then return to you and your future self.

"Why don't you take a break from chasing him?" I propose. "Just let him be and see how things go for a little while?"

"Isn't that what I've been doing all this time here?" you blurt, frustration bursting from every word.

"No, it isn't. All this time you've been ready to pounce on the next lead and take off in frantic pursuit. Even though there haven't been any developments, your state of mind hasn't changed much besides becoming discouraged. Mentally, you're still in track-down mode. I think you should shift out of that for a little while. I'm afraid it'll destroy you."

You seemed eager to rebut my assertions, but that final sentence—murmured as though it could have been an afterthought—is followed by a rapid change in your expression from restrained confrontation to thoughtfulness.

"You know," you begin, voice slow and quiet. "It's kind of odd how I haven't realized that caring about him so much has made it easier to overlook how much you and I care about each other. But I suppose it's not that odd at all, sadly."

"Then again, you could say that being able to overlook our feelings for each other is affirmation of their robustness. We can forget about them from time to time because we know they'll still be there."

You laugh a little and remark, "That's a nice way to interpret overlookability."

I smile at your comment.

"Thanks for letting me be a part of your present," you tell me unexpectedly.

"Glad to have you here."

And we start back in on the springbean salad, enjoying it silently and unhurriedly.